JANICE E

Janice Elliott was born in Derbyshire and brought up in wartime Nottingham, the setting for her bestseller SECRET PLACES which won a Southern Arts award and was also made into a prize-winning film. She read English at St. Anne's College, Oxford, left a career in journalism for full-time writing in 1962 and now has twenty-two novels to her credit, her latest being CITY OF GATES. In addition to this volume of short stories, she has also written five children's books. Consistently acclaimed by the critics, she has been described as 'one of the best novelists writing in England'.

Janice Elliott and her husband now live in Cornwall which inspired her novel THE SADNESS OF WITCHES. For many years she was a fiction reviewer for the *Sunday Telegraph*. She is a Fellow of the Royal Society of Literature.

Janice Elliott

THE NOISE FROM THE ZOO

and other stories

First published in Great Britain in 1991 by Hodder and Stoughton, a division of Hodder and Stoughton Ltd

Sceptre edition 1992

Sceptre is an imprint of Hodder and Stoughton Paperbacks, a division of Hodder and Stoughton Ltd

British Library C.I.P.

Elliott, Janice
  The noise from the zoo.
  I. Title
  823[F]

  ISBN 0-340-56542-X

Printed and bound in Great Britain for Hodder and Stoughton Paperbacks, a division of Hodder and Stoughton Ltd, Mill Road, Dunton Green, Sevenoaks, Kent TN13 2YA. (Editorial Office: 47 Bedford Square, London WC1B 3DP) by Clays Ltd, St Ives plc.

Contents

Acknowledgments

'No Man's Land', 'The Perfectionist' and 'The Saint of Islington Green' are published here for the first time. The other stories in this book were first published in the following: 'Silence', *Listener*, July 1986; 'The Tourist', *Harper's Bazaar*, 1958; 'Divine', *Harper's Bazaar*, March 1963; 'The Actress's Daughter', *Woman*, August 1982; 'Death of a Poet', *Harper's Bazaar*, 1960; 'The Little Monsters', *Harper's Bazaar*, April 1964; 'Fairy Tale', *Best of Fiction Magazine*, J. M. Dent, 1986; 'Interview', *Penguin Modern Stories No. 10*, 1972; 'Figments', *Third Bumper Book of Ghost Stories*, Pan, 1978 and *Midnight Ghost Book*, Barrie & Jenkins, 1978; 'Trystings', *The Twilight Book*, Gollancz, 1981; 'Hymeneal', *Penguin Modern Stories No. 10*, 1972; 'The Interior of Henry', *Queen*, November 1967; 'Body and Soul', *Queen*, May 1967; 'A Friend of the Family', *Nova*, June 1965; 'Reflections', *The After Midnight Ghost Book*, Hutchinson, 1980; 'Going Home', *Winter's Tales*, Macmillan, 1979; 'A Question of Identity', *Transatlantic Review*, Spring 1961; 'No Time for Tigers', *Harper's Bazaar*, 1959; 'The Serpent she Loved', *Winter's Tales*, Macmillan, 1990; 'The Noise from the Zoo, *Penguin Modern Stories No. 10*, 1972.

1

No Man's Land

'Look over there,' she said, 'was that Saudi Arabia? I never could tell where the border was, even in the old days. You remember, we used to ask and they would never admit they didn't know.'

In the hotel at Taba by the Red Sea, she was sitting, wearing her violet silk with the matching slippers and all her ropes of crystal, by the big window in the bar.

They met here every evening at the same time to watch the transfiguration of the mountains on the other side of the Gulf as they were suffused first by a violet the colour of her dress and then by a holy rose, before the sudden desert night obliterated them entirely. They called this the Light Time, not only for the beauty that announced the coming night but for the one tiny illumination each told the other they could see on the shores of Arabia. At first, they speculated about the source of this nightly light: if there were, over there, on the sandy skirts of Arabia Perdita, a hand that threw a switch. Or was it merely automatic, a fortuitous glitter left over after the end of history?

They did not talk about it so much in the last few years, perhaps from the fear of which neither spoke – that there would come an evening when the mountains would be extinguished and there would be no light. Then it might happen that there would be no dawn either. They had dreamed of this. It was possible that it had already happened and they were only dreaming of each other, of this last hotel, of those who inhabited it or passed through it, of the Light Time.

9

They called themselves Leonie and Paul, names they had plucked from the hotel register before it was largely devoured by ants. Not that they had any way of knowing if these names were their own.

This was after the last of all the wars, after sandstorms had buried the dead and their machines and habitations, and the winds had combed the deserts into waves of forgetfulness.

Before the desert winds linear time too had sighed and swayed and without breaking, settled into loops, quite calmly. So it was not unusual for Leonie and Paul to hear sounds of battle or to see a distant caravan. Sometimes, between the siesta and the Light Time, they would make their way to the glass-walled room at the top of the hotel that had once been the night-club. Occasionally the pianist would be playing, couples, unknowing that it was not yet night, dancing or flirting or preening their rich silks and wonderful feathers at the art-deco tables.

Once Leonie said: 'Look, there's Regine.' But mostly the place was empty, sand lay deep on the dance-floor, between fallen chairs, broken furniture and rags of faded drapery from which they could shake the husk-like bodies of locusts. Leonie dreaded that one day they might enter the room at the moment the locusts swarmed through the smashed window-pane.

Otherwise, they had the night-club to themselves, except for a musky scent, the last sigh of a cocktail tune or a leftover laugh.

One day, through the binoculars, they saw a group of pilgrims on their way to St Catherine's monastery. The Sinai was so close it fingered the beach where they lay in the mornings.

They saw dhows setting sail from Aqaba and to the north, a Mig fighter swooping over the Negev. Paul said King Solomon had his iron foundries there and the Children of Israel had passed that way. Would pass that way if they were lucky, if they kept watching long enough. Crusaders too, in their own fold of time.

Meanwhile, there were the Egyptian and Israeli border controls and between them, no man's land. Sometimes. A dirt road between the high rock-face that edged the desert and the sea. The border shifted. One day it might not be there at all. Another, it might be a closed frontier and Paul and Leonie would watch tanks rolling up from Eilat, to the north, and Egyptian armaments and men from the camp to the south of the hotel.

'Oh, good,' Leonie said, 'there's a coach!'

Wavering in a haze of heat and time a package tour was arriving. Or rather, it had arrived many years ago.

For Leonie such visitations meant that the hotel, which was itself necessarily Protean, blinked and woke. The winds of time sucked out the sand and the dead locusts, all the colours and the furnishings throughout the hotel shuddered and were restored, the air-conditioning made Leonie shiver and she clung to Paul's arm as they made their way downstairs. She glittered, she wanted to dance, she would dance later, she would make the wildest love.

'What is it?' she murmured as she lay, her hair spread across his belly.

Paul shook his head. 'You can't go with them. And they spoil the Hour of the Light.'

He dreamed that he would have her here forever, to himself, they would live like this, mariners shipwrecked outside history.

Her secret dream that she would never tell, was of one day following a party of visitors onto their coach, through no man's land to Israel, or even across the desert to Cairo. He guessed this and feared it, though she had never told him.

Meanwhile, for as long as the hotel functioned, they raided the kitchens at night, laying in stocks of bottled water, tinned food and booze. Paul indulged her. They dined in the Omar Khayyam restaurant, watched the belly-dancer from Cairo, ate goat on a skewer and while Paul sulked Leonie flowered. She adored them all and they adored her: the Japanese, the Germans, the Swedes, the Australians, the Brits up from a refinery in the Gulf, the Americans.

She had her hair done, she passed an afternoon with a born-again Christian from Bible Tours who lost his faith and begged her to go back with him to Birmingham.

Although she knew it to be impossible, Leonie was tempted. The boy was so beautiful and, since he had put

11

away his faith for her, as tireless and delicious as a virgin.

'I have given up my immortal soul for you,' he said.

Leonie sighed.

'Tell me, what date is it?'

'The fifteenth, I think.'

'No, I mean what year?'

'Nineteen ninety-one, of course.'

Just as she had feared. She shook her head, kissed him tenderly, slipped on her silk wrap, edged round the collar with feathers from the armpit of the ostrich, and told him the truth.

'Today, I am probably young enough to be your grand-daughter.'

'I don't know what you mean but I can't bear to lose you.'

Paul had starling-black hair and skinny shanks. He was a wonderful dancer. Leonie teased him that he looked like a gigolo. His appearance belied his intensely serious nature.

This boy was, by contrast, shortish, almost squat, his thighs sturdy, his shoulders well-muscled, his whole body hirsute with the finest golden down. Even his flat feet fascinated Leonie. They struck her as immensely practical for every-thing but dancing, so much more useful than Paul's sensitive arches.

Before they parted, they stood together at the window, gazing out.

'Is that Saudi Arabia?' he said.

When she got back to their suite Paul was sulking.

'You missed the Light Time.'

While Paul was in the bathroom a flattish parcel weighing almost nothing was delivered to their door. Inside, wrapped in tissue, there was something shimmering and nacreous, the shape of a fish yet dry to the touch. When Leonie stroked it, it shuddered then rested again. She knew what it was even before she read the boy's card.

This is my immortal soul

Leonie slipped it into her velvet jewel-bag.

In the morning she embraced Paul and said: 'I shall be with him for a few days but I shall love you for ever. He gave up his immortal soul to me. That is a responsibility.'

12

Paul sipped his coffee and nodded. He was not happy but he knew he had time on his side.

Leonie and the boy made love. They ignored the noisy pool with its fantasy island bar and made their way every morning down to the beach. They lounged under the trees – palm and acacia – and Leonie pointed out the beautiful bird with the strange rising call, the oleanders that gave off their scent only at night.

He told her his name but she did not care for it.

'I shall call you Leo.'

Leonie warned Leo not to walk on the coral. They swam from the jetty or hired flippers and masks to swim under-water. The coloured fish dazzled. One time they surfaced between a pair of laughing dolphins.

Leo said he was going to Jerusalem.

Leonie sighed. 'That must have been so beautiful.'

Leonie taught him not to ask questions. She told him only that she had been at Taba for a long time and that she had trouble with her memory. The answers she would not give him stayed in the air between them and became, for him, mysterious night flowers. Some he pressed between the pages of his Bible, for remembrance of her.

He wondered all kinds of things about her. If she had some fatal illness of which she would not speak. If she might be mad. In that case, he adored her sickness and her madness, just as he worshipped her long silver hair and her violet eyes. Also the small mole below her left breast and the shadow that crossed her face when he spoke of leaving.

'Who is Paul?' he said.

Leonie put a finger to his lips. Hush.

'Someone I have known for a long time.'

On the last evening everyone had gone to a party in the wadi. Leonie and Leo watched the gunboats going home to Egypt and Israel and Jordan, and then at the Light Time they lay in each other's arms.

Leo said: 'If you will not come with me I shall stay with you.'

She would not have this. She loved him and wept and pulled on her wrap and paced the room. She pulled at her rings and smashed a glass against the window. She snatched off her crystal beads and they fell to the floor around her, winking with malice, holding their own light.

At last Leonie made up her mind.

From the penthouse balcony Paul watched at dawn. The tour leaders were clucking, the coaches dozed and grumbled awake. In the distance, the Israeli border guards checked their submachine guns. This side of no man's land, an Egyptian emerged from a trailer shed, scratched himself in the groin and the armpits, yawned and lit a cigarette.

The coaches started up, they had already passed the Egyptian check-point when Leonie ran after them. She seemed to be running forever, to be running, bare-headed, through an element as thick as water or time, calling for Leo, until something in the air slapped her back, winded her, and she fell. And falling, heard before she saw, the detonation. It was like a star exploding, the coach, the way the coach blew up.

Time would clear the wreckage, dispose of the dead, the exposed intimacies, the broken doll, the boy, for this was an outrage that happened long ago.

The hotel went back to sleep. The air-conditioning fell silent, without its busy filters the pool would soon stink again.

'It is like a wall,' Leonie said as Paul tended her so gently. Witch hazel for her bruised face, antiseptic cream for her cut lip.

'I know. We knew.'

Neither could have said how long had passed when Leonie got up and made her way from the penthouse to the beach. Although she had no reflection, mirrors watched her.

Barefoot, she walked through the sand and in the brief dusk, at the edge of the sea, she opened her velvet jewel-bag and flung something that looked vaguely like a fish as far as she could throw. Then, with wonder and surprise, she touched her belly, where a secret lay curled.

The holy rose was gone from the mountains. Paul came down and they stood, arm in arm, until night fell from the sky.

The people had gone. Waiters no longer flitted between the trees, the wadi was silent and the sands reached down a little further, towards the time when they would wash over the hotel itself in a forgetful wave, quietly claim this last beach-head, stopping eyes and ears.

At the Light Time, Paul and Leonie clung together. For the first time, the shores of Arabia Perdita were dark.

1991

2

Silence

Who is this girl?

I have tried to write other stories, but she won't budge. She is blocking the light.

It always starts like this:

It is autumn. I walk from the carpark between high fences to the building. For some reason, this first time I have taken care with my clothes, putting aside the colours I normally choose and settling on dull, grey, needlecord trousers, a sweater I don't like very much and a gunmetal cord jacket with big pockets which Liam bought me once. But it doesn't go with anything. No handbag. An old canvas duffel bag Tom used to take camping. What am I after? Anonymity?

What else can I tell you?

At home I think I have a newspaper cutting. In the press photograph she is turning to yell at someone (Her captors? Her enemies, anyway) so that her mouth appears as a black hole, screaming at the world. The filthy sweat-shirt, tangled hair, clenched fist. All bones – but then she had always been thin. People have said this, anyone who knew her, and there is evidence. In my bag I have a photograph, colour, slightly out of focus, in which she must be sixteen or so. Sail-boarding, laughing; her long, brown hair sunbleached and held back by a blue band. She might have been fifteen. She wears no wetsuit, but jeans cut down to shorts, and no shirt. Her breasts are bare, very small. There is something perfect here, an equipoise: the relationship between the girl, the wishbone, the sail, the sea, the sky, the universe.

16

When I show her the photograph she takes it, studies it for a moment as though she were trying to recognise the subject, turns it face down and resumes her seeming contemplation of the bare tree sketched against the small square of sky. (Are there bars? Yes, I think there are.) I have no idea what tree it is until spring, when it should bud. It could be a silver birch.

Someone must break the silence.

I hear myself.

'What do you think that tree is?'

'Have you got any cigarettes?'

'Of course.'

(When did I think to bring cigarettes? I don't smoke myself.)

This will become a ritual. I put down the pack of Marlboros on the table. She will never comment, but some time in the next fifteen minutes she will pick up the packet and hold it in her hand for the rest of the session. She does not yet smoke in my presence. She is probably not allowed matches. I wonder if she ever actually smokes the cigarettes, or keeps them for barter.

It must be a good sign that she has asked for the cigarettes. She has acknowledged me.

After the shock of hearing my own voice I begin to see us.

She must have a name. Shall we call her Judith?

This first Judith I see will not speak, except to ask for cigarettes. Having seen the newspaper cutting and the photograph I hardly recognise this Judith. Expecting a thin girl, I find a fat, pale, young woman. She wears the long, brown hair in a plait fastened with an elastic band, jeans and a sweat-shirt too tight for her since she put on weight. Perhaps it is the one in the newspaper.

The room is an exact square. I can see it now. It is forming. The table is rectangular. A small coin of sunlight lies on the table between us. Once, she touches it with her finger – the only movement she makes while I explain who I am and my reason for being there. (I can't hear my voice – is there glass between us? I seem to have retreated to the corner of the

17

room from which point I see myself as very small, small as a child, the room weirdly expanded and elongated, the two figures very distant at the far end. Will someone take down this damn glass? Or is it water? It seems to flow.)

Then, there I am, sitting at the table again. Judith holds the coin of light for a moment in her hand, palm upwards, but when she notices I am watching she withdraws her hand at once.

This first time she looks bored, a sulky child kept in at school. She makes no sign, even when I ask if I might bring a tape-recorder.

I say: 'Do you want some books? Is there anything you want?'

I say: 'I am allowed to bring you clothes and magazines.'

After fifteen minutes I say: 'I would like to come again.'

Judith shrugs as she makes to stand. That is the most she gives me. And at last a look. Or perhaps she is not looking at me but across my shoulder at the tree sketched against the sky in the square of window.

If I concentrate, what I remember most clearly from that first meeting is the silence. Not of the place: there were doors banging, a sound like a trolley, someone shouted and shouted again until they were answered. But in the silence I left between us, Judith's silence, I felt that she was talking, telling me all kinds of things if only I could hear.

As I left, walking to the carpark, I was startled by ordinary things: the redness of a double-decker bus, small boys playing the first football of the season. A bonfire in the corner of the playing-field which was at once all the bonfires I have ever seen and yet amazing and very beautiful.

That impression is as strong as a memory, a fact.

Real life. Oh yes, let's get back to real life.

Let's say I have made spaghetti and salad. I am sitting at the kitchen table between my husband and my son. That's my husband – the architect, big, sandy man, the soul of reason. Yet he goes to an osteopath called Whitehorn to have his back corrected. Whitehorn says Liam has lumbar distress. There is a lot of distress around nowadays.

'Wake up, Ma.' Tom's talking. Oh yes. Good. He still talks to us, so things can't be so bad. He's all cutting angles – elbows, knees, chin, vast, tall, towering, grinning down at me. Make him smaller, a soft, cradled infant in my arms in a garden. (The violet lids, the hands and eyes expressing astonishment at the created world: Adam's innocence.)

What is he talking about? A trip. An invitation from a colleague of Liam's. He can go to America next summer. Just the fare, if we can manage it. Oh, I should think so. The infant climbs from my lap, he is a giant, he is taller than me, he walks out of the garden and sets off down the road to America. He does not look back.

There is that feeling again. The liquid glass, Liam and Tom on the other side. When windows have not been renewed in an old house you can see how the glass is thicker at the bottom. It runs downwards.

(It is quite possible that this cosy domestic scene is not real. That I have no husband or child. That after the meetings with Judith I go home to a flat. It is painted white, with pine-trestle desk, lithographs, plants, stereo. I tend to over-water the plants. There are brown blisters on the monstera. I sit at my desk to make these notes about Judith. It is queer how she has put all other realities in doubt when she herself may be no more than a fantasy. I don't mind. I don't mind living alone.)

I thought at one point that Judith might be a terrorist and I a reporter. Well, a journalist. I am not so sure now. She is in some kind of trouble, certainly. There is the newspaper cutting. My role could be to help her, if she will be helped.

At the third encounter there is a scene of some sort. That's interesting. I'm encouraged. She is coming to life. I hurry home excited to play the tape. There is a slash of rain on the windows. I live now in a house made of glass, on a hill. It is getting dark a little earlier. From where I sit behind my double-glazing I can see my own lamps and spots reflected in the blind, glass walls. And below, across a black chasm, the

19

street-lamps and the lights snapped on in windows where I imagine people going about the business of life. They have no problem with reality. It is there, in their hands, in a white plate, a blue cloth, a gravy stain at the corner of the cloth, a child's tricycle dropped in a square of light from the kitchen window. A curtain is pulled. The tricycle disappears. It is no longer an image. I blink. The lights are washed away. In their place there is a dark, coniferous forest. Sometimes on a Sunday I will take a walk. The fire-breaks make paths. I was lost there once. It was frightening. In that forest no birds sing.

Just as I sit down with a sandwich and a whisky (what am I doing with whisky? I don't drink spirits) and switch on the tape, the telephone rings. Hell. Who am I now?

. The voice might be coming from underwater. Or someone is speaking with food in their mouth or a handkerchief over the mouthpiece.

'I'm sorry. I can't hear you. Who's that?'

There must be a fault on the line.

If there is a bad connection they will report it. If they really wish to speak to me. If I really live in this house. (I do, surely: I can see my reflection, I can see someone's reflection.)

There is nothing on it but the scrape of a chair.

Then she speaks.

'Why do you always sit behind glass?'

'I didn't know. I'll get them to take it away. Can you hear me?'

I remember. Something is making her angry. There's more life to her face. Apparently I've brought her a twig of winter jasmine. I'm wearing a red jersey dress, my favourite, because I'm on my way to a party. A mohair coat. Scent: expensive smell. It must be close to Christmas. There was a small artificial tree in the reception hall. This room is undecorated, but it has changed shape: now small and rectangular, just big enough to contain the table, two chairs. There is an observation grille in the door. Although it is behind my head I know that every ten minutes someone passes and glances in. Authority of some sort. Warders? Nurses?

It strikes me it was tactless to turn up dressed for a party. Yet why should I pretend I have no life of my own? Parties to go to, family, friends, lectures to give, a story to write, a goose to cook. For the holidays we always go to the cottage. It's a long drive but worth it, even now Tom's gone. It'll be fine just with Liam, of course it will. Tom is in data-processing in Fort Worth, living with a girl I've never seen. Her name is Lee and she has those long, American legs. They eat out, or Tom does the cooking. He wouldn't mind. She's fantastic in bed, oh, how she sings out and laughs and knows little tricks! He might ring tomorrow. Last time he tried there was a bad connection, I thought of all those dark winter waves and different clocks between us, but most of all the Atlantic winter sea, Tom's infant fingers – the last sign to go even after the tender veins so close to the surface of the skin – clinging to the curve of the earth. He is scared of the sea. He was.

Judith can hear me, but there is some great grudge. It comes out at last because she is angry with me for wearing red.

'Where am I? What am I doing in this place?'

It's a wonder she can hear me. My voice is very faint.

'Where do you think you are?'

A scratchy patch on the tape. Somewhere I have learned interview technique. The minimal, simple question, then silence.

'You tell me! You know. You put me here!'

A telephone. A door. Thin thread of a carol from another room.

I am large, tall as the room. Judith is the small one now, just a furious midget yelling up at me. Skinny again. She has been on hunger strike. How can I stop this? They will force-feed her. Just a girl, that's all. Do I love her?

'You fucking tell me who I am or I'll break this glass!'

She picks up the chair and flings it against the glass. Nothing broken, but we are equal now. The room must be soundproof. It is nine minutes since anyone looked through the grille.

'I'm sorry. I don't know enough about you. I should never have come. Perhaps after Christmas, in the spring, I shall know what you were, where you came from, what you did or

21

what was done to you. Then you will be free. I suppose.'

Her hands are pressed against the water-glass; mine too, on my side. Her rage has emptied. In this story, this is the closest we will get.

I go back just once more, in the spring. They are used to me now and nod me through. I was right about the tree: it was a silver birch. Judith has lost so much weight she is hardly more than a scribble in a chair. How could I ever have thought of her? I ask for the daffodils to be given to her and she sits there, the flowers bleeding in her lap. There is no point in apologising any more.

In my house on the hill I have found ways to break solitude into fragments that do not hurt. Bright cushions. More plants. A cat making a puddle of warmth in my lap as I wait for someone to come, to telephone. In my file there is a photograph of a girl sail-boarding, laughing; her long, brown hair sunbleached and held back by a blue band. She might be fifteen. She could have been my daughter.

Last time I played the tapes there was nothing. Silence.

From the housing estate below youths emerge, keen as dogs, to range the evening. They rev their bikes. Yip yip. They wear masks and helmets. They flaunt for the girls and rip upwards, up the hill.

A stone strikes my window. That's real.

1986

3

The Tourist

'It's splendid, perfectly splendid.' The tall man standing
among the blue flowers, surprised, looked first around him
then down at the dark water which lay in careful channels
between the fountains. But neither the earth, nor the stones
of five hundred years ago yielded a sign; the voice in the
Generalife that had assaulted the quiet air came, it seemed,
from no visible body. He shaded his eyes with his hat to look
into the blackness of the arches, but seeing nothing turned
back half amused, half irritated. He had almost forgotten the
disturbance when he was forced to turn by a sound much
nearer, pitched lower, but this time meant without doubt for
him.

'But this is fabulous; oh yes, it's the best so far. I guess you
don't get much better. This silence though, it's fearful, it
makes you want to shout, to break it.' The girl was standing
between the cypresses, apparently as unconscious of her own
beautiful position as the cruelty of her voice in that garden.
Although she looked from the shadows, and so saw more
clearly, he felt absurdly in the stronger position – as the
firstcomer who had already had this spot for half the afternoon; at the same time he wondered that this should matter,
to add up sums of advantage with an uninteresting young
American tripper. And yet surely beautiful, perfect anyway
half-seen against the old trees of the Moorish kings. He did
not want her to move for fear she should break the unbeliev-
able arrangement of pale face on slender neck, elongated to
exactly the right degree by black hair worn straight, the

23

whole shadowed to olive by a disappearing avenue of green. He could just pick out the badges of Rolleiflex and Washington Irving, expensive sunglasses swinging from her hand.

'I surprised you,' she said, with neither apology nor offence, rather as a statement of fact that appeared to her altogether natural. As she spoke she moved out of the shadow past him to lean against the wall; her voice no longer seemed harsh: perhaps he had only imagined it discordant, thrown suddenly and unasked from among the cypresses. With a curious unwillingness to meet her question he hesitated, and together they strolled up to the *mirador*; they looked over Granada to the walls and towers of the Alhambra.

'It is very lovely,' the Englishman agreed; he expected, but did not entirely receive the pleasure of agreement on a beauty indisputable, yet still surprising. 'Yet there are sounds – the water; and those, of course, always.' From the court came the wearily important voice of the guide, predatory bird-like cries of the tourists.

'You are not then, one of them?' Her face was half averted, was she laughing at him? He smiled.

'Why yes; but a lapsed one – I do nothing to support the guide. And you?'

'Oh yes, I am a tourist.' She spoke the words as a lesson learned long ago and remembered precisely, but with indifference. 'What is the name of that valley?'

'The Darro.'

'Would you be kind enough to hold my book?' Every other woman he knew was fussed by a camera, but this girl took her picture quickly and with certainty. It gave him still a moment to observe her; the raised hands were slender, unvarnished, ringless. She wore a bracelet just above the elbow, a plain circle of gold, and her skin had the whiteness which is found most often not in the North, but nearer the sun where the light seems to draw all colour from the pigment of certain complexions. The photograph was over so soon that he felt himself caught prying, when she turned suddenly and smiled:

'Granada roll three; Andalusia roll ten; Europe roll Heaven knows – thank you.' She held out a hand for her book, put on her sunglasses, and as they walked away from the *mirador*, between the fountains, she looked back once at the Sierra.

Since that afternoon in the Generalife he had seen Eloise perhaps five times, now and then in the town when finding her alone in a café, he had sat beside her and talked till the abrupt Mediterranean dusk made it suddenly night. He speculated on the somehow perfectly natural phenomenon presented by the rich young American girl whose very assurance is her passport to travel alone. Adjusting that first picture of her, unsubdued by the Sierra, he began to suspect her of bravado, as though her arrogance were not in fact so sure; there seemed to be a certain anxiety wrapped up carefully in the tissue of precise note-taking, the well regulated but never rigid ordering of her days. Once or twice, at the entrance to a church, the crest of a hill, he felt certain she caught her breath as though to say 'now, surely now – '; but always, under the golden wings of the great baroque angels, at the summit, there was a small failure. Not for some time did it occur to him that this might be a dangerous restlessness. Even when he glimpsed the possibility of evil the vision was so brief and astonishing that he wilfully dismissed it.

He was an idle tourist, a fact from which in this case, he profited. While Eloise, cat-like, prowled conscientiously among the mosaics of the Alhambra, recording, touching, questioning, it was the girl he observed. One afternoon he went to look for her. He had expected to find her at the hotel and, alarmed to discover his disappointment when she was not there, strolled through the town – he told himself, without direction. Still he found her, and once again was arrested by a picture which, if it had been arranged, he would have thought too stylised, too perfect. With hands folded, like the central figure in a triptych waiting composedly for God, she sat between two Moorish arches laced and filigreed with carving, and giving behind onto darkness. As he came nearer very quietly, he saw that while the hands seemed folded, they were locked, the illusion of serenity more like a heavy hooded panic.

'Eloise'; her look when she turned at his voice was, for only a moment, more than surprised, chaotic.

'How clever of you to find me.' With her words the after-noon again became ordinary, the expression he had imag-ined placed in his mind as a trick of the darkness.

'It was so hot – and not a sliver of clean ice in this town. I thought it would be cool here.'

She talked that afternoon for the first time about herself. As they wandered through the town, aimlessly towards the dried-up river bed: 'I was born in Boston, lived there most of my life. Came to New York for a winter after I'd graduated. Then, now, the Grand Tour. Very ordinary.' Ordinary – too ordinary, he wondered. Was she asserting her normality a little too strongly? What in any case did it mean to him that she had something to conceal?

'Why did you come alone? Any special reason?'

'Only that there is so much, and to come alone is somehow less – confusing. You think I'm mad?'

'No, not mad, just crazy.'

As they laughed he put a hand under her elbow and they paused for a second in their slow walk. Then, for that mo-ment only, for the first and last time he considered the possibility of loving Eloise. But they stepped from the shadow of the narrow road, and the early evening crowd in the main street interrupted his thoughts. These considerations were finally to be arrested by a speed of events he could never afterwards remember without shock.

The party that night on the hill of the Alhambra could hardly have failed. Vicente was a delightful host – James had met and liked him once in Oxford on some cultural del-egation. Eloise was to go with him, but finding he had to go to a shop at the far end of the town, he sent her on ahead. When he arrived the party was already noisy and overflowing onto the terrace; he walked in and stood for a moment in the perimeter of darkness where the edges of sound were blurred in the quiet of the garden. He walked around for a while, glass in hand, searching unhurriedly for Eloise. Inside the open windows he could just make out Vicente, garrulous as ever, perched above a group he had bullied or attracted to surround him; the Spaniard was talking, talking, gesticu-lating high as though to pick more words out of the twilight and then more.

The figures around him were attentive shadows, probably strangers to each other, but drawn by Vicente into a circle, like obedient schoolchildren. Then the ring broke as a girl in white silk leant sideways and back to take a light. She was laughing very softly as she held the cigarette to her mouth, so quietly that the Englishman felt only he could hear – and the hand behind the lighter lingered for just a second against hers as the flame became a glowing tip. He had a swift impression of a white shirt cuff with a heavy green link, short strong fingers, squarish nails; a slender, almost translucent olive hand which held the cigarette with the curious determination of a rather old child. Then someone shouted 'candles' and a great branched candelabra, its horns tipped with light, put the garden in darkness and with it the man who had watched. And he saw that the girl was Eloise. He began to push his way towards her and as he spoke, she turned and caught his hand, the only time she had voluntarily reached out to touch him: 'James,' she said, 'this is Manuel.'

They left the party, the three of them, very late, with Eloise as he had never seen her before. In the darkness she was incandescent, a figure that could not have been less of the landscape, and yet was perfectly natural swinging with long strides among the roots and black plants of the hill. For, leaving the house, she had led them not down into Granada, but up higher, to the Alhambra itself. The two men were less than shadows as they followed a flash of white silk, a sound of laughter or a stone dislodged, up the hill into the tunnel of trees. They hardly spoke, except once breathlessly, when they lost sight of her for a moment, and the Spaniard stumbled. James struck a match to see the path, and for a second he glanced at the young man's face; but before he could read in it anything more than the excitement he had already sensed, the light went out and there was a cry from above: 'Quickly, it's wonderful up here. Come on, you've lost me, lost me – ' Manuel raced ahead, and James, arriving breathless at the top, found him circling bewildered among the precise beds and hedges. By night the Alhambra itself was all Gautier could have wished, so formidable that the gardens lost power to it, their daytime formality obscured and foolish. Suddenly their unspoken question was answered, as the walls dissolved into a laughing figure.

'Manuel,' she sobbed, 'Lord, you were funny – look you've crushed the flowers, they're dead – oh Lord.' As Manuel knelt among the star-shaped flowers and tried clumsily to repair their bed, James was reminded of her voice in another garden; but before he could see her face, she too had fallen on her knees. 'They're spoiled,' she said, wonderingly, 'quite spoiled.'

For a week he saw her always with Manuel; the Spaniard was, it seemed, a novice in the bull-ring. He had not fought that season because of an injury which had put him of necessity out of training. James knew little or nothing of the *corrida*, and was amazed and impressed by Eloise's understanding – he knew for a fact that she had seen only one fight, in Madrid. But then this strange girl, always remarkable, had suddenly become spectacular. She dazzled; yet she never again obscured the Spaniard, drawing him rather, to sit quiet but never foolish within the circle of her brightness. He was in fact a very ordinary young man, but with Eloise he seemed surer, his English unhesitating.

Only once, when Eloise was late, and James talked alone with Manuel, was he reminded of the night on the Alhambra and the young man stumbling, an unwilling clown among the flower beds. He talked for a while about the prize-fighting life of the *corrida*, the career of the *torero*, not unlike a boxer's, rich, spoiled, short. They were sitting in a café, Manuel at ease, adored by the waiters as a local celebrity, even though his name set up in Madrid only the faintest of murmurs. Then, as the patron, proud to have captured Granada's own *novillero*, lingered by the table smiling for an order, the Spaniard turned: 'All right José, that's all we want.' It was almost as though he had dismissed the waiter so that he, the worshipped, could discard his authority and become, with sudden reversal, the suppliant.

'I am going to New York,' he said, 'with Eloise. And we will be married.' Then he slapped the table with his hand, starting the waiters like rabbits from behind the hanging beads, till they stood around him, scared but enquiring.

'Drinks for you all, and cigars for my friend.' Laughing, he seized the bewildered José, and kissed him on both cheeks, then threw out his arms as though to encircle them all in a huge embrace. Just then James caught sight of Eloise, who had come unobserved down the hill towards them and paused, watching, at the corner of the street. Unwillingly, but because he liked the man, James found himself regretting that she should have seen.

He saw them after that, almost every day – yet never Eloise alone. He felt she was in fact avoiding him. Once he thought he had trapped her, on an excursion up the Sierra. As they panted in the thin air near the snows she fell behind and rested on a rock. He sat beside her and they smoked as they watched the figures of the others, diminishing against the mountain.

'So you are going to marry him – '

'Yes.' She leant back against the rock, her eyes closed, the ash growing on her cigarette.

'You are going to New York – he wants that?'

'Manuel, he wants it. Oh, yes.' She sounded tired, yet some curious nerve forced open her eyelids.

'When will you go?'

'In a month perhaps.' The girl moved her position to watch the disappearing figures. 'But first there is the *corrida* at Linares on the 17th.'

'The 17th? That's the big fight isn't it, he wants to see it before you leave?'

'He is fighting in it.' She jumped to her feet as though to shake off the conversation, and began to walk quickly along the path. He ran to overtake her, and seized her arm:

'But he's out of training; he's not well and he's a novice not ready for Linares. Even I know that he shouldn't fight – he'll lose his reputation and he could get badly hurt.'

'I know nothing about bullfighting. But Pedro Jiménez has broken his leg and cannot fight. Manuel is the best *novillero* in Andalusia; his agent has fixed this fight. After Linares he will be a *torero*.'

'If he isn't dead.'

She walked on still faster, by now gasping for breath.

'He must realise that far better than we do – does his agent

29

approve?'

'Manuel persuaded him.'

By now they had almost caught up with the rest of the party:

'You want it?' The question had suddenly become urgent. As the others saw them and shouted encouragement lost in the air between, he repeated it: 'You want it, don't you?' Manuel was waving from the top of the mountain, and she waved back.

'Yes, I want it.'

In the town his fears were confirmed. Manuel was already a dead man in the cafés and squares. Until the afternoon before the fight he did not see them again – Eloise took good care. Instead he walked the streets, and went up once to the Generalife, already chilly in the late afternoon, the air above this fabulous garden less golden and the fountains blown to spray by a breeze. He stayed only a few minutes and came down the hill to see Manuel's big car waiting in the square. José stood shyly beside it talking to Eloise in the front; in his hand was a great bunch of autumn flowers, the tissue rattling in the wind that piled leaves against his feet. Then he pointed and waved the bouquet excitedly as Manuel came running from the café with his agent; a photographer pushed through the small crowd that had gathered, and a barrage of flowers hit the fighter. A dog began to bark hysterically, and from the crowd someone shouted, 'There he goes, just like a bride – ' He never reached the car. A bus, turning into the square hit him first on the legs and then, as he put up his hands to shield his face, on the chest.

Almost the last James saw of Eloise was that afternoon in the square. She did not bend down to Manuel, but stood, slightly hunched, her face as empty as disappointment.

Towards the end of that winter he wandered, from the cold of Piccadilly into a bar in Jermyn Street. There, by chance, he heard as much as he would ever know to complete the story. She was sitting alone, huddled in furs, and when she saw him smiled apparently without surprise, almost as though she had been waiting for him. But still she said:

'What are you doing here – I thought you were always in

Oxford. But it's wonderful to see you.'

'Not always.' He sat down opposite her, and for a while they talked of Oxford, of London, and nothing. It was she who said:

'I go around still you see, but soon I'll go back.'

'Back – ?'

'To the States. Go on, ask, go ahead.'

'He lived?'

'Yes. They had to amputate a leg, but otherwise he has made a wonderful recovery.'

'You didn't marry him?'

'Marry him – ' She still had the habit of repeating a question: she seemed to try the words as though they were new to her, and any interrogation a little surprising.

'No. Oh, no.' She picked up her gloves but made no move to go. Then, as if she would never stir, she leant back against the wall, her thoughts turned in, he felt, on some vision she could hardly contemplate, and he would never understand.

'To be run down that way, by a bus, like a jaywalker – the fool, the poor fool. When he could have died so perfectly.'

It was the first time he had seen her cry; he could not remember afterwards what he said, but he left her and hurried out into the mist. As he walked towards the park, he thought that whatever sacrifice she was looking for when he first met her in the garden, it had in some way failed her.

1958

4

Divine

The two women rode into the village at sunset on the backs of donkeys. The donkeys wore straw hats with holes cut for their ears and the women, too, shaded their faces with very similar hats, but elaborately decorated with real flowers, now faded and drooping; the younger of the two women (for as they came closer it was apparent that their ages were widely separated) was particularly hung about with flowers, nose-gays tied at her throat and garlands at her waist. Yet they compelled not laughter but silence for there was about them an air of elegance, so that they wore their flowers like jewels, and, by the straightness of their carriage, ennobled their donkeys to elephants at the head of a royal train. And there was indeed a follower, a young man who puffed behind, fanning the flies from his face with another of the wide straw hats. As they rode past the café, their donkeys stirring up the dust, it could be seen that they were wearing a striking riding gear: an elaboration of silk, in sunstruck, breathless colours, which hung as a straight tunic down to the waist and then split into billowing trousers, caught again at the ankle.

When they had finally disappeared round a bend in the street, in a cloud of dust turned by the sun from dirt to a honeyed gold, as if they carried with them their own atmosphere, the man who had been watching put down his drink.

'And who the devil are they?'

The barman, together with the rest of the street, those walking and sitting, those watching from windows, and even the dogs, who did not bark, now stirred as if from an enchantment. The dogs began to run and yap again, the walkers shrugged and went on their way, and the sitters, in windows and doorways, continued to weigh the alternative pleasures of conversation and sleep, a problem which would never be resolved until death at last took from them the one and gave them an eternity of the other.

'Those,' said the barman, crucifying a fly on his forehead with the flat of his hand, 'those are the Divine ladies.'

'Divine?' Hugo looked after them as if expecting them to reappear, manifesting themselves again in a cloud of gold. 'You mean they're saints? Divine?'

'Saints,' said the barman and laughed all over his body, rolling with laughter and upsetting the flies and calling out across the bar to tell the street, 'saints. Oh no, not saints. To be a saint you have to be dead – ' he crossed himself as anyone else might sneeze ' – and Mrs Divine is alive. Saints.' He spat with precision over his shoulder.

'That's their name then? Divine? Are they all called Divine? Are they a family?' The older woman, he supposed, was the mother, and the younger, who resembled her not in feature but in bearing, the daughter. The man might be the son. Or a servant. On the whole, he thought, a servant.

'All of them,' said the barman, holding up three fingers to indicate his meaning, 'all Divine.' He relaxed his fist and then started again with two fingers. 'Both ladies, Divine. And he too, the man, Mr Divine. Three.' He raised a thumb to join the two fingers. 'All Divine.'

Hugo had come to this uninteresting village because it was neither smart, that is to say comfortable, nor uncomfortable enough to be in another sense smart. He had chosen Spain because he had been there before and he required, at this moment in his life, a place that would not bother him, give him any surprises. At home, familiarity was painful. There were too many places in which Mildred had refused to marry him, and one in particular in which he had realised, quite suddenly, that he did not in any case want to marry Mildred. He was treating himself as a convalescent for whom France was too expensive, Italy too exciting. So it had to be Spain, and of all places in Spain, this one, where nothing could ever happen. At the bend in the street there still hung a cloud of gold. It was, he thought, no more than a trick, a trick of the sun, sun and dust.

He was invited and accordingly he went in the evening up the dry path, full of brittle noises, the cracking of twigs and desiccated chafing of cicadas, a long hot walk to the top, where in this higher place there was a suggestion of air and a faint coolness of pine. From below he had seen the pines but not the house which revealed itself only at the last turn. Once fine, it had surrendered itself to flaking plaster and the advancing ruins of a garden in which dull pale little flowers and laurel had themselves given way to a relentless scrub.

After the sun, the hall was an aquarium in which he swam, conscious of the cold of marble at his feet, the pond-green light through shutters which gave to everything the drowned and shimmering look of underwater life; and there was the true sound of water, very close.

'You like our fountain?' Hugo saw first the fountain, probably a natural spring imprisoned in the house, so close it was a wonder that he had not stepped straight into the marble bowl; and then at the furthest end of the hall where the light, for lack of light and because of a certain gold on the walls or the ceiling, thickened to amber, Hugo was aware of a thin young man who seemed not to have arrived but materialised with startling suddenness out of this very amber darkness. Hugo had a feeling that if he went any further and stretched out his hand he would be able to touch the air like treacle, or a river-deep mud in which was sunk a shoal of golden fish.

But the young man's hand was cool. 'Divine,' he said, as he must have done a hundred times, with an air of faint apology, 'Derek Divine.'

Hugo had expected a party, or perhaps one or two others, but not to be alone like this with the three: the young man, and those two women, who after greeting him relaxed in their cane chairs as though they would never speak again. The older Mrs Divine had indeed not risen at all by so much as a degree from her position among silk cushions which were arranged to support and comfort every part of her body so that she made of the attitude of resting not just a convenience but a positive luxury.

In the odd silence after a glass had been placed in his hand, she seemed to be watching him like someone who had set a play in motion, and waits now for it to begin. She was decorated this time not with flowers, but with real jewels, a fantastic assembly of diamonds at her ears, garnets at her throat and all other kinds of winking, heavy treasures from her head to her waist, and even a thin chain of pearls round her ankle. Perhaps that was why she rested, from the weight of the jewels pressing her into lethargy against the cushions of silk. There was a scent in the air like incense. Hugo wished he had not come (as a Methodist, Mildred had abhorred incense above all other manifestations of the Virgin's Church, and he, he supposed, had caught from her this rather unreasonable horror). But it was not incense; a joss stick burned, one small taper filling the room with its curling scented smoke. When the old woman spoke, Hugo realised that while she had been watching him, he in his turn must have been rudely examining her.

'They're not real you know'; her voice was a surprise, hoarse like a man's, but not old; 'fakes, the lot of them.' She thrust a finger at the younger woman. 'Daphne detests them. An old woman's fancy, my silly bits of paste. Eh Daphne?'

'Darling.' The younger woman seemed about to get up, to make some gesture, press the old woman's hand, in some way lovingly reproach her, but she thought better of it. 'Our visitor,' she said, 'will think us very rude.'

'Not at all,' said Hugo. 'Paste or not, I think your mother's jewels are remarkable. She wears them very well.'

For the next half hour they talked and the occasion took on, at last, a semblance of normality. The joss stick died, Hugo's glass was refilled, a lamp was lit and the room which had been dark, became, as night filled the garden, the lighter place from which, as they murmured like moths around the lamp, they could see the young man Derek as a shadow in the garden, returning now and then to the window, then like a gardener occupied by roses, he would vanish again to stoop mysteriously over some triumphant weed.

Hugo was aware of a powerful communication between the two women as if a thread joined them, invisible but very strong; and with him on the stool at their feet, they chose to toss him the thread and from time to time to make it quiver

35

beneath his fingers, to pretend that they were taking it from him and then, so gently, to return it. He was struck again by the resemblance between them which grew stronger, he thought, as the evening progressed, until he decided that it was certainly physical, more than a trick of the light or a matter of bearing.

He realised, as he was about to leave, that they had allowed him to talk about nothing but himself; an experience which now embarrassed him but left him all the same with a pleasant sense of importance. They had drawn him out, displaying their interest each in a different way, the older woman with quick little movements of her hands, like jewelled birds in the air before her, the younger with smiles. The more he told of his ordinary life the more they let him feel that he had enchanted them; he even talked about Mildred, and then he was drowned in smiles, the birds flew and the thread danced at his fingertips.

When the girl had gone to light a lamp in the hall he felt that he must, with some courtesy, thank them.

'Your daughter is very beautiful,' he said. 'And the resemblance between you is outstanding.'

The old woman clucked and threw down a silk cushion from her lap like an animal she had suddenly found a nuisance. She answered looking, not at him, but out into the garden.

'My daughter?' she said. 'Oh no, sir, not my daughter. Daphne is not my daughter but the wife of my son. The two Mrs Divines. Now go, go, I'm tired.'

Before he could get to the door she seemed to be sleeping. He saw Derek in the garden, still standing among the weeds, and Hugo thought for a moment that he was coming forward to speak. But the young man shook his head very slightly as if in answer to a question, raised his hand in a half-salute, and turned back to the house.

After that he saw them almost every day, and while the framework of each occasion, the shape and colour of their meetings, remained much the same, he discovered each time a deepening affection for these two women, and an understanding of the differences between them, which seemed only to emphasise their ultimate affinity. Daphne, for instance, was shy. They would talk for a long time in low voices, he and she, while the elder Mrs Divine slept on her cushions, but once when he laid a hand on her arm, to stress a point, she suddenly withdrew it with a look of such challenging innocence that she all the more bemused him. At the same moment Mrs Divine awoke, and in the simplest, most childlike way, Daphne crossed the room to kiss her and the two clung together, wrapped for a moment in a private and touching exchange. Hugo thought of Mildred, who rarely embraced even her own mother of flesh and blood. His own was dead but he could not imagine that, if they had met, she and Mildred would ever have had much to say to each other.

Once or twice Derek joined them, and when he did Hugo could not think why he stayed away so often.

'Here we are, the three of us,' said Mrs Divine, quite forgetting Hugo, 'and who else in the world do we need? The best thing, my dear Hugo, is to live like this, in your own world.' And Hugo believed her. He only envied Derek, whose arrival implicitly banished Hugo from the magic circle; and yet there was something odd about the young man, for whom Hugo felt at the same time sympathy and irritation. Sympathy because of his mysterious lifelessness, which suggested not so much illness (if he was ill why was he not in bed, or in hospital?) as the absurd possibility that his spirit, his ghost in the old first meaning, had been taken from him; irritation that Derek showed no sign at all of relishing his position as the husband and the son of two exceptional women. Hugo felt that, in his place, he would do better. Which reminded him, not for the first time, of something that had troubled him the last few days.

When he did kiss Daphne, in the end, it was as he had expected in the middle of the afternoon, when Derek had gone off to sleep upstairs, and Mrs Divine too slept, the only evidence of her slumber the faintest exhalation from her lips which barely disturbed the air. The kiss itself was hardly more violent, but it satisfied Hugo. But when he came to think about it afterwards, it was not the kiss he recalled, nor the fact that Daphne seemed ready and delighted to accept it, but a glimpse he had across her shoulder of Mrs Divine nodding in her sleep, as if someone had made a remark with which she entirely agreed. Many years later Hugo remembered this occasion, and the moment, too, in which he discovered in his own mind, a speculation which was no more than a seed in a dark place, that if Derek were ill, and were to die, he himself might not be unwelcome in this house.

The fire was spectacular, and the whole village turned out to watch the flames devour not only the house, but the surrounding pine trees, which burned with an aromatic scent like incense. It was best seen from the sea, and some of the observers went out in boats; they reported that the entire hill appeared to be burning, and that, at its height, it had the look of a pyre.

The barman used his telephone to call the fire brigade, first wiping his hands on a cloth. He told Hugo that it was a tragedy, but at least there was a comfort in remembering that one of them would have died whatever.

'You mean Mrs Divine? The old woman? She seemed to me remarkably well for her age.'

Not Mrs Divine, but the young man Derek. His disease was incurable, but unspecified. The barman had seen something like it before, or rather his father had seen it, in the mountains where there was no priest – the barman crossed himself not once but twice – and the people, the women leading the men, made their own religion. Some men had died and finally an expedition was sent: a priest, a doctor, and half a dozen Civil Guards, one of them the barman's father. From when he came back to the day he died, he was never entirely himself again.

As he watched the house consumed by fire, Hugo thought of the two women spinning their thread in the scented night. Which of them had said: 'I cannot imagine how we would do without Derek. There is no proper home without a man about the house.'

'Well,' said Mildred, scratching her stomach as she lay beside him entirely naked except for the new gold ring on her left hand, 'what I think is that they were mad.'

Hugo studied her practical little body, quite familiar, but very pleasing.

'But it was quite an adventure, wasn't it?'

Mildred sighed. 'Oh yes,' she said, 'divine.'

1963

5

The Actress's Daughter

Always, every year, she would go to the beach before breakfast, before it could be spoiled; and the first morning was
best. To wake to the seagulls' screech and chatter, dress, leave
her parents sleeping and claim her bay. Rosie would antici-
pate this all the last, weary, chalky days of school, and this
year more than ever. Nineteen thirty-nine was a hot summer.

'Tregower' was her secret incantation: 'Tregower, Tregower.' A word that was a spell to summon blinding sea-light,
veils of fine rain the sun would sweep aside, the crack of the
tide in an unseen cave, the small beached anemone and wild
eyebright, the soar and tumble of gulls off the cliff-face that
had appeared to Rosie once to be the windy edge of the
world.

To be the first to walk barefoot in the sand after the tide
washed it clear was to make the first prints in snow; she had
never before been too late.

She wanted to turn back or run past the rock where the girl
sat.

'I thought no one would ever come. My name's Nerissa.'
Uninvited, the stranger slipped from the rock and walked
beside Rosie. With her bright yellow skirt and floppy straw
hat, she looked like someone dressed up to go to a beach.
'Where are you staying? Have you been here before?'

'Every summer since I was small. We stay at Lamorna, that
guest-house in Fore Street.'

'Poor you. We're at Pirate's Place. We usually go abroad.
My mother's an actress.'

'Pirate's Place? But that's the one round the point on the beach – it's been shut up for ages. It's beautiful. I used to pretend I lived there. There were some people once, ages ago – they had a big white car and they used to sit on the terrace in the evening. They had a party – I can remember the music!'

'That was probably Angela. My mother – she's been before. It's not so bad. You can come if you like.'

'Shouldn't you ask your parents?'

'Oh, Angela won't mind. She never does.'

'Is she very famous? Would I have heard of her, do you think?'

'I expect so. Angela Storm. She's resting at the moment.'

Rosie nodded quickly. She supposed it must be tiring, being an actress.

Abruptly, Nerissa turned away.

'I'm going back now. Come for tea. I say, what's your name?'

'Rosemary.'

'Rose-marie!'

Rosie wondered if she should shake hands, but Nerissa's mother was lying in the garden on a long chair – more like a bed – with a white fringed canopy lined in green. She wore trousers that looked like beautiful cream silk pyjama bottoms. Her hair was tied in a chiffon turban and she seemed to have a ring on every finger.

In a deckchair by her side sat a man in a striped blazer and a younger man lay at her feet, cravat at his neck, white flannelled legs crossed. It was as though a Hollywood film star or a bird of paradise (much the same thing really) had alighted in the garden of Pirate's Place.

When Rosemary said, 'How do you do, Mrs Storm,' everyone laughed and Rosie coloured, wished she had not let her mother put her in the checked gingham dress, wished she had never come. But Nerissa's mother smiled and shushed the others.

'Oh, my darling girl, they're all idiots, take no notice. It's Storm for the stage, you see – silly name my agent thought up. There he is, getting too fat in my deckchair – Colonel

41

Archie. And this – ' she tipped the young man's shiny yachting cap over his nose ' – is Jock.' She waved her hand. 'Nerissa
– before Rose-marie starves on her feet, get her some pop or
whatever you children drink nowadays.'

Rosie followed her new friend into the kitchen, low-ceil-
inged and cool after the August heat outside. Nerissa found a
bottle of lemonade and took a biscuit-barrel from a
cupboard.

'Oh, Lord, silly old Archie's forgotten to get biscuits. D'you
mind?'

'No. Just a drink, thank you. It's so hot.' Rosie was uncer-
tain whether or not the other girl really wanted her there – as
though Nerissa had invited her and now could not think what
to do with her. But Nerissa said: 'You can stay, can't you? For
the evening?'

'I'm not sure. They have tea at Lamorna. Sort of supper, I
mean.'

Nerissa raised her eyebrows. 'How funny. Well, telephone
them then. But do stay. It's so dreary here with no one to talk
to. I can't talk to Them. What do you want to do? I don't like
swimming. It messes up my hair. The water always gets inside
the cap.'

Rosie thought that was sad, not to enjoy the sea. 'I haven't
brought my bathing-suit anyway. But I'd like to see the
house. It's lovely. I used to pretend I lived in it. Which is your
bedroom?'

'The little one at the front. You can see it if you like. But it's
just a room.'

'You don't know about the spy-hole?' Nerissa shook her
head and Rosie went on as they climbed the stairs. 'Well, in
the old days, raiders used to come not just from France but
from other harbours in Cornwall. A pirate called Brown Dog
lived here and when there was warning of a raid he used to
keep a lookout through a spy-hole. He used it to watch for
excise men, too – this was a famous place for smugglers to
meet.'

Even Nerissa seemed impressed. 'How d'you know all
that?'

'The guide-book.' Rosie smiled, then Nerissa laughed
properly for the first time since Rosie had met her. She

looked quite different – pretty. Rosie searched along the bedroom wall. 'Look! This stone lifts out and it's narrower at the other end.' She stood back. 'Put your face close up to the wall.'

'Ugh. Spiders. Oh, yes! You can see them all in the garden but they can't see us. Archie's gone to sleep – like a walrus. And Jock's pawing Angela. I wish he wouldn't.'

Rosie was embarrassed. 'Isn't Jock your father?'

Nerissa hooted. 'No, thank God, nor ever will be. He's a scrounger and Angela dotes on him. Archie says he's a bounder but then I think he's a bit soft on Angela himself, really.'

Rosie digested this, impressed. She had never seen a real bounder before.

The evening was fun. They all sat out in the garden, looking over the low wall at the beach and the ebbing tide. Rosie was shy but fascinated by Jock, who mixed pretty coloured drinks in a cocktail shaker. Nerissa had one but she pulled a face and drank it like medicine. Rosie refused.

'Taken the pledge, eh?' Jock was very brown and his teeth were very white. Rosie blushed and shook her head, hoping he wouldn't tease her. When he just smiled and said nothing, she liked him better. Perhaps she could see why Nerissa's mother doted, though she seemed rather old for that.

'What about din-dins, then?' Angela said. Colonel Archie came awake, like an old dog from its basket, shuffled off, and came back after fifteen minutes with a heaped plate of wild-looking ham sandwiches – jagged, as though they had been cut with scissors. Perhaps they had.

'No pâté?'

'Sorry, Angel.'

'Oh, well.' Angela smiled indulgently, forgiving, and with her beautifully manicured scarlet nails tore the clumsy crusts from the sandwiches. Rosie thought they were actually very good and said so to the Colonel.

He pulled his gingery moustache and bowed from the waist. 'Thank you, my dear young lady. Thank you very much.'

A flurry of herring gulls screamed around their heads, swooping to snatch the crusts, terrifying Angela, who waved her arms and covered her head. 'Archie! Jock! Nerissa! Do something!'

Nerissa sighed. 'Oh, Angela, for heaven's sake.'

It was Colonel Archie who scattered them, flapping his Panama hat, though not until every last crust had gone.

When it was time for Rosie to go, Angela was charming. 'Do come again, darling, if you can stand us silly old dodos. Perhaps we'll have a party. Yes, let's!'

Nerissa walked part of the way along the front towards Lamorna. It was a soft dusk, full of scents, the brilliant colour of the daytime flowers now muted, except for a white, waxy flower that glowed like a candle.

As they parted, Nerissa said: 'How long are you staying?'

'It's usually only a week, but we'll be here for three this time. My mother's been ill – she's better now, but the doctor said she ought to have several weeks by the sea.'

'Do you have to stay with her?'

'Oh, no. They spend most of their time in deckchairs. Rather boring.'

'Then will you come every day?'

Rosie was startled but flattered. 'I'll have to ask, but I expect they won't mind.'

As she walked away, she turned back and saw Nerissa watching her. The other girl appeared suddenly lonely, a little sad.

'I think you're wrong about Jock.'

Rosie had finally got Nerissa in the water and the two girls were sitting on a warm rock with a view in one direction out to sea, in the other of Pirate's Place. Nerissa turned her head to look up at Rosie. Already dark-skinned, she tanned beautifully, olive all over. Since Rosie had got her swimming and rock-climbing, she had lost the old sallow, sulky look.

Rosie went on: 'Honestly, I think he's in love with your mother. He never leaves her side.'

Nerissa flopped back on her towel. 'He says it's too cold. Never swims anywhere but the Med.' She glanced again at Rosie.

'I say, you've got a crush on him, Rose-marie!'

'I have *not*!'

'You're blushing.'

'You pig! I'll drown you!'

The weather held. Rosie took Nerissa to explore her favourite bays and was glad to see that she seemed happier. When they were together like this all day, she no longer cared if she cut herself on a rock or got salt water in her hair. One day, when they had taken a packed lunch supplied by Lamorna out to the furthest headland, they lay in the dry grass on the cliff-top. Rosie pointed out the blue finger of another promontory.

'That's the most southern part of England, of the mainland, at least.'

Nerissa didn't answer for a moment. Then she said: 'I'm happy here. It's so beautiful.'

Only when they returned to Pirate's Place did Nerissa become preoccupied again. Rosemary wondered what upset her friend. Perhaps, in spite of the front she put on, she didn't like her mother doting on a bounder? As for her father – Nerissa remarked casually one day, as though she sensed Rosie's curiosity – he had 'scarpered' with the 'ingénue' in Scarborough. Whatever that meant.

The day of the promised party everyone at Lamorna gathered in the landlady's parlour to listen to the wireless. They were all talking about war and some were packing up to leave at once. At Pirate's Place Rosie found Colonel Archie paddling at the edge of the sea, with his trousers rolled up. Seeing Rosie, he doffed his Panama. 'Rotten thing this,' he said, 'rotten old thing.'

Some friends of Angela arrived, rather noisy, everyone kissing and shrieking. In the kitchen – which held no more than a table, chairs and an awful range – Rosie helped Nerissa and Archie to make crab sandwiches.

'Come on,' said Nerissa, 'don't go back to change. You can borrow one of my dresses and I'll make you up.'

Rosie wasn't sure about the make-up. She supposed it would be all right if she washed it off before she got back to Lamorna. As for the dress, she was thankful not to appear in the wretched gingham. The two girls laughed at the startled reflection of the made-up Rosie.

'I've only had lip-salve before. And Yardley Rose last

Christmas.'

'You look a little cracker, as Archie would say.'

At the top of the stairs they regarded each other, smiled, and Nerissa impulsively hugged Rosie. 'This has been the best summer,' she said, 'the best holiday.'

Someone had hung Japanese paper lanterns in the trees. Archie, winding and winding, kept the gramophone going ('I like a nice tune'). Rosie drank two little green drinks that looked and tasted like peppermint. She danced twice with Jock and shivered. At first she was stiff, then he talked and made her laugh, and she relaxed. Nerissa was right: this was the best summer.

Looking for Nerissa, she went indoors and upstairs. Not finding her in the bedroom, Rosie sat down for a moment, nodded at her new face in the mirror, then idly pulled out the stone and peered through the secret peephole.

It was like looking down on a stage, lit by moon and lanterns. The music played on and perhaps only Rosie saw Angela and Jock in the far corner of the garden, shielded from the dancers by the tamarisk. She could see that one was speaking urgently, and then the other. Then Angela drew back her arm and slapped Jock across the cheek.

Just as Rosie had reached the foot of the stairs, Angela ran in and brushed past her, sobbing painfully, as though to cry hurt her physically. How ugly she looks, Rosie thought. She went to find Nerissa, but instead she told Archie: 'I'd better go. They'll be waiting up for me. It was lovely.'

Archie was the last one Rosie spoke to and in the morning it was he she found on the beach, standing among the jetsam of the party – broken glasses, a crumpled paper lantern just above the high-tide mark, a woman's sandal. He was abstracted and for a moment appeared not to recognise her.

'Ah,' he said, 'our little Rose. What a rotten thing.'

She knew he didn't mean the war this time.

'What's happened, Colonel? Where is everyone? I've brought back a dress.'

'They've done a midnight flit, you see. Scarpered.'

'Angela and Jock?'

'Eh? No. Jock and Nerissa, bag and baggage – well, Angel's

best bangles and petty cash. That's to say, endowed themselves with all my lovely Angel's worldly goods.'

'Oh, Archie!'

The Colonel straightened his back. 'Ah well. We'll be off. Find ourselves a winter lodging somewhere – Hove, I daresay.'

Rosie knew now: Angela's 'rest' was permanent, the Colonel was probably no Colonel. And love? Would she ever know about love?

She laid the dress on the low wall and, on an impulse, kissed Archie's cheek. She walked slowly away from Pirate's Place. From a distance it appeared as perfect as it had the first time she ever came there.

1982

6

Death of a Poet

The day that Jim Shepherd said he was going away, everyone bought him a drink; not that this was unusual, for as the local poet he was accorded in the pub the indulgence normally allowed to very old dogs or young children. No one knew why he and Francie had come to Gospel Oak, but if they had hoped to set themselves up as rarities, they had succeeded. There wasn't another poet within drinking radius of the Hog and Litter, and the only one who did call from time to time frequently sold his work, and so was expected to stand the beer himself. I lived there because it was cheap, and I didn't mind much where I lived, but you would have imagined that Jim and Francie, who were sensitive, might have preferred to be among their own sort. Jim would sit for hours by the shove-halfpenny board, and sometimes Francie would join him, winding her long legs round each other till we used to say that's what a heron would look like if it came in and sat down. Twice in the evening she would go behind the bar to ring up the children. Brutus was seven and had a phone by his bed; once he telephoned her because Cassandra had toothache, and Francie loped away taking a bottle of Guinness, which she said would be better than aspirin.

The children were remarkably well behaved considering everything. Brutus looked after his tall blonde mother. I've seen him walk down the road behind her, picking up the hair-pins that fell from her coil of golden hair. It was lovely hair. Little Cassandra was too small to look after anyone, but she did the best she could not to get in the way. Once I met

Francie in the nearest she ever got to a terrible state. She wasn't crying, but hopping from foot to foot, and her hair had come right down. She clutched my arm like a saviour.

'Cassandra,' she said. 'I've left her somewhere.'

We went through the shopping list, and found her in the end in the greengrocer's lap, playing with a potato.

I liked their house in a way, though I never felt quite right in it. It was one of those little villa places, more like a country cottage, and they had knocked down most of the inside walls. The builder used to say it was a miracle that it stood up. Where the walls used to be, they had hung sacking, which Francie had painted with strange colours and shapes. The place was full of clocks, mostly under glass domes, but at least half of them didn't go. It was queer to look at them all set at different times and speechless under the glass; one of them had been mended but lost a hand, so if you knew the hour of day you were all right for the minutes. There must have been about thirty owls in the house, all in glass cases so that you couldn't sit down without an owl looking at you, like old women behind windows. Then Francie read in a magazine that stuffed birds can get some disease or other, and bathed them all in TCP, putting them to dry in the airing cupboard, where the cleaner found them and gave notice from fright. Most of their feathers fell out. Up at the top of the house there was a small room which Jim kept to himself; the children weren't allowed there, though I'd been in once. It was quite different from the rest of the house, almost empty, with only a table and chair, and a mattress on the floor. Jim said he did his writing there, but whatever went on up there he always seemed a bit depressed when he came out, and he always came out at opening time.

The time he sold a poem to an American paper called *Come*, which was printed in Paris, there was a party at the pub; the children came, Cassandra in a sling on Francie's back, like an Eskimo, and Brutus walking. They were allowed to sit in the landlord's own parlour, to make it legal, and drank Dubonnet and lemonade, which wasn't legal. He showed us the poem, and I didn't find it too difficult to understand, though I did wonder why the lines were all different lengths, until he explained that it was three-dimensional poetry, to be read to yourself, to be listened to, and to be looked at, so the shape had to be different. In the end it was never printed, because the magazine closed suddenly, but by then Jim had got the money, so it didn't matter.

They weren't a couple who showed their feelings much, yet you knew they were all right. Francie was a wonderful cook, and over their food they made a funny sort of love, in the way that other people do by holding hands; Francie would put down the plate in front of Jim as if it were a present, and after a mouthful or two, Jim would look at her softly, and they would be exchanging some private message.

When he said he was going away some of us nodded, some smiled, but I put down my drink because there was something a bit sharp and special in his voice, as if it were important.

'On holiday?' I said, wondering where he'd found the money.

'In a way,' he answered. 'But I won't be seeing you for a while.'

The others had gathered by now that there was something going on, and raised their noses, like dogs, from their drinks. No one said anything, but you could feel their interest concentrated on Jim. They were waiting for him to explain, but when the silence got so thick you could have smothered in it, someone said in a loud voice:

'Well let's have a drink on it then.'

It turned into quite a party. I went to ring up Francie, and she came along with Brutus and Cassie. It was warm enough to prop the pub door open, so we put them on the doorstep.

When Jim had downed two pints and a chaser, I drew him to one side:

'What's it all about then?' It was after all his own business, but I couldn't help feeling that on the strength of the drinks, we had a right to ask.

'It's a sort of experiment,' he said. 'I can't tell you about it, but it's something to do with a theory I've got.'

'Anything to do with your poetry?'

'In a sense. You go along like this for years,' he said, waving a hand to indicate the crowd around us. 'Then you have to do something about it. To find out something about yourself. I've got to find out if I'm a poet.'

'What about Francie and the children?'

'Francie knows. She agrees.' I thought he was going to say something else, but someone put down a tray of beer in front of us, and he never finished.

I went round almost every day to keep Francie company in the evenings. It was a hot summer with days like ovens that often blew up into a thunderstorm around seven o'clock; there seemed to be electricity all round you, and I got a shock when I touched my car door. Sometimes at Francie's we sat around with our feet in the fridge to cool off, and once we moved out the food and put Cassie in. She chuckled with relief, but I took her out quite soon, because I knew Francie might forget her and shut the door.

We ate out of doors most evenings, watching the green energy gather in the sky, till it looked as if the whole firmament would explode. Then a rush of wind would blow out the candles and we knew we'd have to go in, or get wet. Then we would play records and I'd watch Francie, with Brutus asleep on her lap, and wonder how Jim could have gone away, leaving this.

The room would be full of music, the clocks ticking away under their domes and the moulting owls benevolent shadows in their glass cages. But then it's not the same for everyone. There seem to be some who can't settle down to happiness, and it's not necessarily the miserable ones. You see them enjoying themselves like anyone else, more if anything, but there's a look in their eye, and you know they won't be staying. Jim was one of those.

Whenever I mentioned Jim, Francie found some pretext to drop the subject, fussed over Cassie, or remembered something she had to do. Quite often, if it was after supper, she simply fell asleep. But one night I did say:

'Any news of Jim?' He'd been away for five or six weeks, and apart from anything else, I wondered how she was managing for money. I hadn't got much, but I would have helped. I must admit that when it began to look as if Jim was gone for good, I had thought quite a lot about Francie. Although she probably never imagined me like that, I could see she was getting used to me; with Francie you could go on for hours and think she'd never noticed you, then she would give you one of her smiles, so warm you'd think you were the only person in the room, and feel as if you were drowning.

'Oh, no,' she said, 'no news. But we hadn't expected any.'

'Why do you think he went?' There was no harm in asking. She thought for a moment:

'He wanted to find out if he was really a poet.'

'Do you know where he is?'

'He said something about going to Vic's cottage.' Vic was the one who sold his poetry and used to let out his cottage sometimes, or lend it. Now I thought this was funny because Vic had sold his cottage six months before to a retired light-house-keeper who had committed suicide and burned the place down. But I supposed Jim might have forgotten and gone there anyway.

Then one evening after supper, when Francie had fallen asleep, Brutus slipped off her lap, and took me by the hand. He sometimes did this, leading me round the twilight garden, pointing out his special treasures, attentive as if he had grown them himself.

'Show you something,' he said, but instead of taking me out through the French windows, he led me upstairs. Outside the small attic room he pulled me down to keyhole level, and repeated:

'Show you something,' then, 'See Daddy?'

Incredulous, I fixed my eye to the keyhole. In a pool of fading light Jim was lying on the mattress, hands behind his head. At first I thought he was asleep, but a beam of light suddenly flashed in his eye, and I saw he was staring at the ceiling. Gently, I tried the door; it was locked, and Brutus was tugging at my hand, suddenly guilty. The room was just as I had seen it before, with the table and chair, and one rough blanket was thrown on the floor by the mattress.

Downstairs, Francie stirred from her sleep as we came in. I steered Brutus out into the garden, and pulled the windows to.

'Francie,' I said, 'wake up. I've seen Jim.'

'Oh, dear,' she said, and rubbed her eyes. 'Did he see you?' I shook my head. 'Then that's all right.' She lay back in her chair and looked as if she might drop off to sleep again.

'Francie,' I said, 'you mustn't go to sleep. I want to know what's going on. It's not all right. He looked awful.'

'I told him it wouldn't be good for his health. But you know Jim.'

'But what is he doing there? What's the idea?'

'I suppose I'll have to tell you now.' Francie looked round vaguely, as if searching for something she had mislaid.

'I've put Cassie to bed,' I said, 'and Brutus is in the garden.'

'Oh, he knows all about it. He thinks it's a game.' She seemed to be making an effort to wake up.

'He's been there all the time,' she said. 'He wanted to be alone, but he couldn't afford to go away, and there didn't really seem to be any point in going. He can be alone up there. Twice a day I leave food outside the door. He's not smoking or drinking, so it's easy. He's going to stay there till he's found something out.'

'Aren't you frightened?'

'He'll come down when he's ready.' She suddenly thought of something: 'You won't tell anyone, will you? He wouldn't like that.'

I left early that night, and stood for a while in the street, staring up at Jim's window. It was in darkness, and I wished he'd put on a light. I didn't like the idea of him up there alone in the dark. But when I came to think about it I didn't feel so bad. He'd probably written a lot of poetry, enough to sell.

The next weekend was the hottest yet. I'd been careful not to talk about Jim to Francie, but I could see she was a bit worried, and I noticed that there were several plates-full of food in the larder.

'He's not eaten for two days,' she said. 'I knocked on the door this afternoon, but there was no answer.'

Neither of us felt much like going to the pub, and we were sitting with the fridge door open when there was a shout in the street. Looking out of the window, I thought for a minute, that's funny it's snowing, but it was paper falling from the sky.

'There's something going on out there,' I said, and we all trooped out of the house. Brutus was the first to pick up a sheet:

'Letters,' he said, 'letters from Daddy.'

They were the queerest letters I'd ever read. It was a sort of diary, and when we came to put them in order, with Brutus stationed outside in case any more came down, I got a shock.

They started off with a bit of poetry, and the date that Jim shut himself away: June 29th. The first week there was a page every day, with the date, saying how he was trying to write, then it didn't seem to come. After that there were fewer pages, mostly about the thoughts that passed through his head. He thought of giving up and coming downstairs about the third week. He said how he waited every day to hear Francie outside, and spent most of the time thinking about her coming, and remembering her when she'd gone. Then he began to look at his room, to look at the way the floorboards were laid, and there was a lot about a patch of damp on the ceiling, and some spider or other that always came out at the same time every day. Then he found a bit of broken mirror and looked at his own face; he looked at a different bit each day, and said that the eyes were unbearable. After that the diary missed several days, until a last page where it said that he'd found out what he needed to know, so he probably wouldn't be coming down.

When I saw that I ran up the stairs three at a time. The crowd from the pub were in the house by then, as they had seen the snowfall of paper and come to find out what was going on. Francie was standing in the middle of the hall, Cassandra in her arms, with tears rolling down her face.

As we broke down the door we heard a sound inside like an animal, and someone said:

'Watch out, he might be dangerous.'

But he was lying on the mattress just as I'd seen him, hands behind his head.

'Come on,' I said, 'come on, Jim. Time to come downstairs.'

When I last heard of Jim Shepherd, he had made a fortune out of his diary, which had been reprinted in French, Italian, Spanish, and Serbo-Croat.

1960

7

The Little Monsters

The children ran along the fringe of the tide following their leader, the line only broken, and then not broken, only changed for the moment, when one or another jumped aside from the sea, which was coming in and encroached suddenly in unexpected places. The smallest, at the tail, was inclined to linger over this and that, a warm pool, a ribbon of seaweed, he was anxious to interfere with the privacy of a crab, the beach was new to him, but without pausing in their formal dance the others reached back to pull him on.

The beach was new this morning, a clean tide in the night had washed it, the crab waited for the sun to warm the pool. There were other crabs, and molluscs of all sorts, who had waited and been turned to stone, the beach was famous for these effigies, sea creatures and their accompanying plants companionably petrified. When you came to look closely you could see that the cliff was made of these dead things; it was, if you had a morbid turn of mind, a graveyard.

It was a famous cliff and in the summer its face was hung with explorers, amateur and professional, breaking their nails in a hunt for prizes. Mixing with the bathers and the sea-birds, parties of students in shorts were delivered to the cliff-top by charabancs and turning their backs to the sea – though some would have liked to bathe – they would point their faces at the cliff and write in notebooks. The gulls were used to them, even welcomed them for their sandwiches. Sometimes in the early morning white-robed monks came down and splashed at the water's edge, throwing the sea at one another with sharp cries, like girls, but they had not come this morning. The children possessed the beach.

They found the man sleeping in a rowing boat. He might have been thrown up by the tide, he was so grey, his skin had the greyness of leather which has been in the sea. They watched him sleep.

He woke and saw them standing round him. They were wearing white linen hats and faded seaside clothes. They were only children. If he had a cigarette he could pull himself together and send them away. This was no time for kids.

There were seven. One was no more than a baby, he was pulling at his pants as if he wanted to pee. But the others took no notice. The eldest was a girl, she ought to do something about the baby. They were getting on his nerves, not speaking, he was not used to kids. He was at a disadvantage lying in the bottom of the boat, he must look a mess, you'd think they'd be scared. Run away. Run away kids. He thought of pulling a face, or if he had sweets he could say, go on kids, go away, I'll give you sweets. He could just have got up and walked away, walking first and then running, but he had run himself out.

'Who are you?' That was the oldest girl. She looked more like a boy, flat-chested in a boy's shirt. She was boss.

'Father Christmas.'

She turned to talk to the oldest boy. It was a meeting. The faces of the children were empty. If he ran now – they blocked his way to the cliff path – he would run into the sea. He had swum last night from the next bay and he could still taste the salt in his mouth. Running and swimming, he had had enough, he had hoped only to lie here in the bottom of the boat for a while, for the sun to warm him up a bit. He was not ambitious. Time enough for decisions when he was warm.

The meeting was over. The girl's sandy hair was bleached almost white, there were freckles all over her face, she must have been here all summer. They probably came here every morning.

'Are you hungry?'

Food. Kids are quick sometimes. They know. Perhaps it had been lucky after all. If only they would not give him away.

'Yes.'

'You're starving aren't you?'

If only they wouldn't stare. He didn't have to admit anything. He was after all a grown man. He had never got on with children. Even when he was a child. It was a relief to grow up, you didn't have to talk to them. Even like this, wrecked, you had the right, being grown, not to answer them.

The oldest boy, not the biggest but clearly the oldest, spoke next. There was a feeling that when one spoke the rest agreed. They did not look at one another, only at him. The little monsters knew what he was thinking.

'If you don't tell us we won't give you anything. We've got banana sandwiches and hard-boiled eggs.'

'All right. Yes. I'm starving.' He could imagine the thin shell peel off in one go, the soft egg underneath, the feel of it slip down his throat.

'You know you gave me a fright.' They were all right really. They had given him almost all their sandwiches and the eggs, out of polythene bags, and a cigarette, bent in half, the boy had in his pocket. They sat round him like dogs and watched him eat. He was safe in the middle of the circle, no one could see him. It was really, it really was, he thought on a full stomach, a stroke of luck. The boy watched how he smoked, pulling the smoke right down into his lungs. The man became suddenly cheerful, a jolly uncle on a picnic, his pocket full of tricks. He might turn out his pockets and show them a penknife, a piece of string. On a good day he would turn his pockets inside out and they would squeal at the half-crowns, dig for them in the sand.

All you needed with children was the knack. He congratulated himself on having, unexpectedly, discovered it. They were like animals really, or nogs. Those nuts who went after nogs, you read about them in the paper, in Africa, just as the locals were measuring your head for size, you handed out the prizes. All lord-like you brought out your watch from under your jumper and the nogs began to dance. Women too. Women, kids and nogs.

They were still sitting round him like dogs, on their

57

haunches. They did not move. But their eyes danced when he turned out his pockets, inside out, and they saw the raw blade of Jiminy, his knife, out of its sheath. Jiminy – he could tell them but he wouldn't. You could trust a knife, keep its face clean and it told no tales. But they liked it, even the dumb blade, they saw its promise. Now he had something that they would like. Better than boiled eggs.

'You want to hold it?'

He did, the middle boy, you could see that. He had eyes for nothing but Jiminy. He devoured Jiminy with his eyes, his hands itched to hold the blade, his thumb in particular to test the edge, for sharpness, for the feel of death. They looked at each other, the man and the middle boy, and understood that the man held death in his hand, very gently, for fear of a loss or an accident. No one said death, still nothing disturbed the bright morning, there was no violence in the little wash of the waves, violence had long drained from the dead sea beasts which clung in fossil peace to the cliff-face. A boat, far out to sea, believed the beach to be empty, it caught the flash of sun on the still blade Jiminy and thought it to be a piece of glass or mirror. Only the children and the man knew who Jiminy really was.

The man saw suddenly a situation which could be turned to his advantage. There was a tenseness about the little group, they had changed their point of view. They yearned, in different ways, after Jiminy, and forgot for the moment the sense of power they had won over the wrecked man. They yearned, with fear and love, for Jiminy, the oldest girl mostly with fear, as if she could see on the blade what Jiminy had done, the boys with varying degrees of desire. The man teased them, holding back the knife while he considered his price. It had been luck really, luck, thinking of Jiminy, turning the tables like that. Who would have thought that kids were such little monsters? Even the man, who had seen a lot, who had been in many dark places and been acquainted with monsters, was shocked. You would think that a man like him, who had known such things, would be beyond surprise.

'Has it killed? How many people has it killed?' They had voices like birds, young birds.

'That would be telling.'

'Where, where has it killed?' 'In the dark.' 'When? When?'

He had never in his life had such power. That was what he had missed all his life, power like this. Until now he had not known what he wanted.

'Who? Who did it kill?'

'Let me touch. Let me have it. Let me. Let.'

They were probably nicely brought up. They said their prayers and washed behind their ears. They had clean fingernails. They lived a life the man had never known. He was seized by a pang of curiosity, as fierce as hunger. He would have liked to ask them questions. What did they have for breakfast? Did they sleep between sheets? But he knew he must keep to the point.

'If I let you . . . ' The only thing that worried him, now he could have anything, was what did he want? He could ask for anything.

'If I let you, will you get me some cigarettes?' That was not enough, he could ask for much more.

'Will you hide me? Will you find me a place to go?'

'First. First. Tell us. Let us hold.'

Anyone who had been watching, like the solitary fossil hunter who had arrived alone, at the top of the cliff, set on a certain special prize he did not intend to share, might have seen that the state of affairs on the beach was not quite what it seemed. From a distance, from the sea or the cliff-top, power lay not in the man holding what appeared to be a knife or a piece of mirror or a jewel that caught the sun, but in the children, powerful with desire.

The fossil hunter saw when they turned on the man, like young dogs or birds, whom hunger drives, and took the knife away from him.

They ran away from him, carrying the knife, along the fringe of the tide which was now almost at its height. Soon, if he did not move, the wrecked man would himself be engulfed by the sea, and taste salt in his mouth. He lay in the position of the dead or the disappointed. Soon the sea would reach the foot of the cliff and unless you knew, you would never dream that there had ever been a beach.

1964

59

8

Fairy Tale

Once upon a time there was a good woman who took her children for a walk in the forest and told them a story.

The good woman Caresse looks up from her typewriter and sighs. She looks at the blue cornflower in the white pot on her desk. She looks around her white room – Oh, the room of her dreams, in the house of her dreams: the high white room (Max calls it her cell) with the rough pine table, the sanded floor, the view of the ocean and the forest, and the plain day-bed. Yes, very like a cell.

Not that Caresse is cut off from the world, indeed. When she is working (especially when she is working well) her mind travels comfortably around the rooms of her house, observing the curve of a banister, counting her children, pausing to gossip with Max in his workshop among the motes of golden dust.

They might have some people in this evening or they might be alone. Sometimes the Millichamps come over, sometimes Caresse and Max go over to the Millichamps. Sometimes they take the children, sometimes they leave them, since the oldest Millichamp and the oldest Stungo are both sensible children and the houses are close enough, with no road to cross between.

Caresse puts aside her neat pile of typing paper, secures it against the breeze from the open window with her owl paperweight carved for their fifth anniversary by Max and weighted at the base with lead. She walks around her room touching her magic objects: the paperweight, the bladder-

60

wrack seaweed they found on the beach, a blue glass bottle they dug up in the garden, and, best of all, the children's offerings: drawings of stick-people (Mummy and Daddy) on the notice-board; a polished pebble, wobbly paperknife, pigeon's feather and jam-jar holding one expiring tadpole – all talismans, lares and penates, bless them.

Caresse smiles, leaves the room, closes the door behind her and calls out: Come on, children, I'll tell you a story.

Once upon a time, says Caresse – walking through the forest telling her children a story – *there was a good woman who took her children for a walk in the forest and told them a story.*

This is an old deep forest – not one of your new conifer conservancies of fire-breaks and nature trails and neat birds. Here are still the tracks and monuments of the dark ages: forest rides like cathedral aisles, towering beeches whose tops are lost in a semblance of infinity. Underfoot the soundless loam of great age and decay and here and there a reredos of brighter green larch or birch. In the black heart of the forest no birds sing.

Wearing her ankle-length sprigged dress, Caresse enters the forest barefoot with her children tugging at her hand. Tell us a story they cry, tell us a story; then they are distracted and run away, for there is a flash of red squirrel, almost extinct. The red squirrel has survived here, Caresse tells her children, because this is a forest on an island. But England is an island? (the planet is an island in space, for that matter). But even islands have islands: to the mainland, which is also an island, came seafaring grey squirrels who are very sweet eating corn on a bird-table but wiped out the red, gobbled up their dinners. Or the grey squirrel may be an innocent scape-goat. Some species are simply inadequately equipped for change and do not survive.

Tell us the story, they say, so the good woman tells them: *as they walked through the forest she told them a story of the woodcutter and his wife and his children.*

Oh, it's a *woodcutter* story.

Tell us a swineherd story!

Tell us a princess story!

Princess stories are yuk!

Still on the outskirts of the forest, Caresse's children dance in the falling flakes of light, squeal and chase and run back to their mother for a story.

Hush, be still, chides the good woman, or I will not tell you a story at all. Look at that greenfinch! A dash of gold then Caresse hugs the smallest to her and steps on into the wood.

In any case, this is not a woodcutter story. It is a story about a good woman, who lived with her husband and her children in a house on the edge of a forest: so close was their house to the woods they could hear a weasel cough or a badger scratch. Deer grazed almost at the front door and on a dusky evening the great white owl flew low past their open window and warned: Watch out, watch out.

(Have you written this story already or are you making it up?

All stories have already been made up. You only have to listen and tell.)

They were a happy family. Every day the husband went off to work, mending chairs, and every day he kissed his wife and all his children; every day he said, as he strode off with his tools in a bag on his shoulder and a good cheese with a whole onion in his pocket: Mind your mother and do not go into the black heart of the forest.

They were a happy family but just sometimes the children quarrelled, as children do. Then their mother wrapped up a goat-cheese and apples from the loft. She looked at the hearth to be swept and the beds to be made, yet she knew that beds get made some time and hearths can be swept any day, and instead she took her children into the forest and told them a story of a woodcutter and his wife and children.

This is the story the good woman told.

A woodcutter and a good woman and their children lived in a hut in a forest. One day the woodcutter's wife took the children for a walk in the forest and told them a story.

Wrapped in a muslin cloth in a basket, the mother, who was a good woman, carried a goat-cheese and in the basket too was fresh-baked bread. One of the children carried the bag of apples and sometimes he slipped behind his mother's back and ate one. His mother knew what he was doing but pretended not to notice.

Once upon a time, said the woodcutter's wife, there was an old wood where children played. You may play there every day, their father said, provided you do not go into the black heart of the forest. (Was he a woodcutter? asked the children. Yes, he was a woodcutter like your father, said their mother.)

(There could be too many woodcutters in this story.)

However. Mostly they minded their father and stayed within sound of the ring of his axe. But one day (said the carpenter's wife telling the story the woodcutter's wife told to her children), the woodcutter's children were so busy playing they did not notice how deep into the forest they had strayed.

What did they meet in the forest? asked the carpenter's children.

They met a talking squirrel who cried come, come on, into the heart of the forest, where a goatherd disguised as a prince languishes by a stream and two black knights fight forever to the death for love of a lady they will never free for she belongs to the forest.

(Neither the woodcutter's wife nor the carpenter's wife knew that what the talking squirrel actually said was: I hate wood-cutter stories.)

The strange thing, said the carpenter's wife, is that as the woodcutter's wife told her story, and as she walked through the forest with her children, they came upon a talking squir-rel and a goatherd disguised as a prince, and two black knights fighting forever to the death for love of a lady.

Real? Absolutely real? asked the carpenter's children.

Oh, yes. As real as you or I or your father mending chairs and the onion in his pocket.

Caresse's children are hungry. They want to peel the story like an onion and gobble it up, all gone. If they were not such good and cheerful children they might eat up their mother for the story inside her.

Was the lady in the wood a princess? A yuk princess?

No, she was not a princess. She was a woman who worked for a living.

Now, says Caresse, spreading her skirt and settling beneath one of those heaven-seeking trees, we will eat our bread and cheese, then you play hide-and-seek or sleep perhaps. And later I will tell you the rest of the story the carpenter's wife told her children.

But it was the *woodcutter*'s wife's story!

Oh, my loves – it was the carpenter's wife's story *about* the woodcutter's wife's story.

(Perhaps I should never have brought in this woodcutter.)

Caresse spreads goat-cheese for the youngest and hands the others their bread, to spread themselves. Then she tells them: the lady in the wood, you see, worked for her living by singing songs she made herself. And everything she sang of came true – the talking squirrel, the goatherd disguised as a prince and the two black knights fighting forever to the death for love of a lady.

The good woman Caresse kisses each child as it sleeps. While they sleep she walks on, in her sprigged dress, barefoot, deeper into the dark heart of the forest where no birds sing. The deeper she goes, the more she is drawn on, brambles snag her skirts and wild roses prick her cheek. There is a flash of red.

About these woodcutter stories, says the talking squirrel.

About these talking squirrel stories, says Caresse.

She hears the ring of iron as the two black knights fight forever to the death for love of a lady, and decides to give them a miss. Deep in the black heart of the forest she meets a lad in princely gear moaning by a stream. He is her secret lover and falls upon her at once, having seen her reflection in a stream.

I am your secret lover! he gasps, bounding upon her.

I am a good woman! she cries, bouncing beneath him.

You are a prince! A prince disguised as a goatherd! Or a goatherd disguised as a prince! You know my secret heart and all my desires! You are all I have ever wished!

Actually, he says, I'm a woodcutter.

*   *   *

Caresse sits up and brushes the leaves from her skirt, the twigs from her hair. She is sitting on a mossy mound, neat as a velvet pincushion. Her secret lover sprawls on his stomach, chewing a straw and grinning. Insolently, she would say, if they had not been one moment before in boundless ecstasy.

You are definitely a goatherd, she says.

If I'm a goatherd you're a princess.

Whose story is this anyway?

It's a lousy story, says the talking squirrel.

Of an even and sunny temperament – known for her common sense – Caresse has rarely felt so put out. Her hair, she knows, looks a fright and when she bends to check her face in the stream, there is no reflection. Only the dark eye of the forest stares back.

What happened next? ask her children, roused from sleep by their mother's return. Normally she loves them like this, warm and sweet from sleep, but today she is edgy as a hedge.

The carpenter's wife – she tells her children – told how the woodcutter's wife and her children played a game with the talking squirrel and the goatherd disguised as a prince and the two black knights, and then they went home. The carpenter's wife and her children went home too. And now we're going home.

What game did they play?

Stud poker. The talking squirrel cheated.

So Caresse and her children leave the forest, which seems no longer so enchanting but a nuisancy place. Caresse sends the children to play with the Millichamps. She drops her ankle-length sprigged dress into the Ali-Baba laundry basket and takes a warm bath followed by a short sharp shower. Then she lies on the day-bed in her white room, her cell, with a sympathetic but not intoxicating yellow drink in her left hand, and her right forefinger resting lightly on her forehead to clear her mind of forests. After a while she calls her husband, Max, on the inter-house telephone and says: the Millichamps are coming over tonight. We'll have a quiet evening and we may or may not play mah-jong. I have had a tiresome afternoon but I'm fine now.

You see, the tiniest adjustment, and equilibrium is restored.

Caresse walks through her evening house, counting and naming the rooms, followed by a sweet trail of thyme and rosemary, roasting with the breast of lamb. In every room she snaps on every light until the house blazes to defy the forest.

And here come Dymphna and Hereward Millichamp – exactly the friends she would have chosen – crossing the clearing to dine with Caresse, who thinks she is talking brilliantly tonight, though actually she is a little drunk (and who can blame her; talking squirrels are a pain in the neck).

Caresse says: Oh, we are so lucky. When I look at the rest of the world and see the things going on, the hijacking and the brain-damaged children and the sexual assaults upon grandmothers and the bad architecture and the divorce rate and the death of the whale, I think we are so fortunate to be together like this without cancer. Do you think there was a touch too much garlic in the marinade? That is such a pretty dress, Dymphna, though I like your blue best, I always like you in blue, I have some blue beads you shall have. I don't think I shall ever leave here. I don't think I shall ever go to the city again. Why people have to run around so in such herds, I cannot imagine, it's no wonder they get trampled. There is, after all, the life of the mind and there are some very good films on television. Why go to the cinema and catch cancer? Max, pour the wine, Hereward, have some more syllabub. Give me your hands! Let us make a vow. I had a silly afternoon in the forest today.

Even in her present state, Caresse's sensibilities are sharp and she can see there is something funny going on. Max is looking at the table. Hereward is looking at Dymphna. Dymphna says: Caresse, we have to tell you that we're moving.

Moving! But you can't move!

I'm sorry, Caresse.

But why are you moving? Caresse is suddenly sober. She sees that her hands are red and puts them under the table. She may take up smoking again. She may drink a lot more or nothing at all.

Dymphna says, as gently as she can: we simply don't feel, Caresse, that there is room in this story for our characters to develop.

This doesn't *have* to be a short story –

I'm afraid that has nothing to do with it.

Dymphna. I have never before begged anyone for anything in my life. A novel? A trilogy?

Thank you for a lovely dinner, Caresse. The lamb was perfect.

But you won't know where to go – where will you go without me?

To tell you the truth, we fancied the theatre.

You idiots! Caresse howls. You'll see, she yells after them – it'll be a woodcutter play!

Towards dawn Max comes to her in her white room. He is faint already, fading fast.

Caresse is cried out. You too? she says.

He takes her hand. They sit side by side on the narrow bed. She always loved his hands.

I would have built with them such wonderful things.

But I was never a carpenter.

Who has custody of the children in such cases?

I don't believe this has ever come up before. I don't know.

When even Max has gone, in search of a novella about a novelist trying to write a novella – when he has, alas, at last, slipped through her fingers into the blue morning – Caresse sits down at her typewriter, sighs, dashes away a tear and begins to write:

Once upon a time there was a good woman who took her children for a walk in the forest and told them a story.

1986

9

Interview

'So what would you do next? Normally, I mean.' The young man was very tall. He walked around the low-beamed cottage. When he paused to make a note or ask a question his pale cotton trousers rode up revealing celery legs. He settled in high places where no one had ever sat before.

'I'd work, I suppose,' she said, then with more confidence, 'I write every morning from ten till two.'

'Splendid!' said call-me-Simon, as if she were a clever child. 'We'll do that.'

'Won't it be a bit dull?'

'Not if we do voice over. But leave that to us.'

'Oh.'

She sat at her desk. She pulled in the chair, put paper in the typewriter and raised her hands. Outside her husband was mowing the lawn, round and round. He was being considerate, she knew, making himself not there. She suspected that call-me-Simon thought Bill was the gardener, and could imagine no way, short of the farcical, of putting this right.

Her face was stiff with smiling. 'I can't think what to write.'

'Just behave normally. Pretend we're not here.' The camera whirred.

She lit a cigarette from the box which was kept filled on her desk, remembered she had a small pride in not smoking on television ('I don't know why but I can't stand women puffing on the box'), squeezed it out, tipped it into the wastepaper basket and pushed the dirty ashtray in a drawer. She waited for the wastepaper basket to burst into flames. She tried to

68

stop smiling but couldn't. Perhaps she would be stuck for life with this idiotic grin. The camera prowled closer, an enquiring bird. I am a watchbird watching you.

She typed:

THE BROWN FOX JUMPED OVER THE
Janet Johnson
Well Cottage
Wishing Green
Janet Craig-Cooper is a lazy dog

'It's silly,' she said, 'I can't think what to write.'

The camera retreated, respectful but implacable, waiting. Janet looked at Bill through the double-glazed picture window. He had finished going round and round. Now he would mow the edges. He made a point of not looking at her. He encouraged her work. He said it was important. Once or twice he had been called Mr Johnson. Janet Johnson wrote cool, intelligent novels about women with domestic problems. Her own life ran so smoothly. She led Simon round the house, showing him. 'That was the bread oven,' she said. 'This is the original fireplace and that's Jacobean. That's my husband out there and this is Matthew.'

'Marvellous,' breathed Simon, 'marvellous.'

Matthew was conservative. He did not approve of anything that was happening today. Such a pity, Janet often said to Bill, that the nearest playgroup was ten miles away. Someone younger to cope with him, an au pair perhaps? But more trouble than they were worth and hopeless in the country. And then he adored Mrs Munnery and next year he'd be at school. A nanny, of course, was out of the question. Mrs Munnery was one thing, but to hand over your child body and soul to another was a treachery Janet could not even consider.

She stooped but Matthew would not come to her. He told Simon: 'I'm four. I was sick last night.'

Simon said it would be absolutely marvellous if they could get a shot of Janet bathing Matthew. He had already been bathed, as usual, by Mrs Munnery when she came in at nine, but now Janet was to bath him again. The idea was so utterly absurd that the vague hysteria which had been rising in her all day nearly broke out. But she was carried away on a tide of arrangements, proposed by Simon. She felt helpless, strangely isolated in her own house, awkward with her child.

Matthew did not care to be bathed. He protested, was bribed and cajoled and finally gave way, but held himself resentfully stiff. He captured the soap and with a foxy smile cracking a face she felt to be varnished, Janet urged him: 'Give the soap to Mummy, Mat.'

Janet sweated. Simon asked from his perch on the lavatory: 'Can you tell us what you are working on now?'

'Give the soap to Mummy, Mat, at once.'

'What do you feel about the future of the novel?'

'Matthew, GIVE ME THE SOAP.'

Simon said vodka. Oh well, yes, then he'd just have a tonic. The crew had gone down to the pub. Janet's hand was shaking. She poured herself a double whisky. She waved to Bill who was squatting on the lawn in the midst of the dismantled mower, happy as a child on a beach. He looked straight at her, it seemed, but did not wave back; it would be the angle of the light. Help! she wanted to cry and gulped half her whisky before she turned to Simon. 'I'm not much good at this, I'm afraid. I didn't really want to do it.'

'Of course you didn't. It's irrelevant.'

'So you do understand!'

Janet Johnson made Janet Craig-Cooper do it. Janet Johnson agreed with her publisher and her agent and her husband that this was just the kind of breakthrough she needed to reach a wider public. Since Janet Craig-Cooper was proud of Janet Johnson she consented, admitted even, with a part of her mind, that she wanted madly to do it. Writers and such who despise sales figures and pull up the drawbridge against opportunities like this, were simply not living in the world. After all, one was writing to communicate, or one should be or one should not be writing at all. I mean one can live in an ivory tower and chuck whisky bottles at call-me-Simon, but might that not imply that one has nothing to say, or worse still, something to hide?

Janet Craig-Cooper knew that everything was not only under control but as good as it could be: happy, healthy

70

child, placid husband, full fridge, poulet au blanc and Gewürztraminer for Simon and Janet Johnson, nothing to do but whisk off the covers and serve.

'Oh well yes of course I've thought about giving it up when Matty was born for instance I wish I could sometimes be like ordinary women if there is such a thing it must be heaven but. Honestly, I think and Bill agrees I'm much nicer if I'm working and being Bill I can't imagine a situation in which I would have to choose Bill says. Of course one's family first if Matty were ill but well yes, one does hope that never.

'Some time perhaps though Bill doesn't feel strongly and I. I have no intention of disclosing to several million indifferent ears the obstetrical details of a perfectly hideous confinement. I couldn't write when I was pregnant, it's quite common. I hated it, I hated Matthew for the first six months of his life. Janet Johnson out in the garden eating worms while Janet Craig-Cooper grew fatter and madder. Not for your box.'

Yet I dream sometimes of the girl even Bill doesn't know about this. If Matty died endlife. Endwork? I truly don't know. Don't ask. Don't look. If Bill.

'Oh yes, Bill is really marvellous, he's so patient. How women manage with a husband who doesn't *understand*. I'm lucky, I know I'm lucky.'

Janet Johnson told a funny story about the only time she and her husband had a row about her writing. He said something wasn't quite up to her best and there'd been this fantastic scene though of course he was quite right, as she realised even at the time which was why she threw the casserole on the floor. And there they were on their knees mopping up pot roast then picking bits of glass out of one another's hands then they both saw the joke.

Janet Craig-Cooper remembered it had not been so funny although it happened exactly as she said. She remembered she had tried to conceive that night or rather not tried not to conceive; and had gone through hell for three weeks thinking she might actually have brought it off. That was Matthew.

The rows we have not had since are the dark places in our marriage where we do not go.

'Marvellous,' said Simon, 'you restore my faith in marriage.

71

The new book?' An autistic child, the strains on the parents, weak father, divided mother, you know the thing. ('To a potentially melodramatic situation Miss Johnson brings her customary subtlety of perception, honesty and wit. All the more moving for the restraints imposed by a formidable intelligence, the compassionately forensic revelations of a writer who is never afraid to plumb the darker, most private corners of human experience.') Have you ever tried to plumb a corner, for God's sake?

'Actually, I did do a bit of research. Those children, you know, it's terribly sad. I felt awful, like a spy.' I sat in on classes for autistic children for exactly one day, after which I drove home very fast and was sick as a dog who's been eating dirt. I did my Belsen wardress act with Matty. By the time Bill came in I was howling, he was so sweet. How could I tell him I was howling for poor Janet who can't see anything nasty without throwing up?

Janet writes about nasty things because she doesn't want to look at them. Writing sends them away. When she had nightmares as a child she used to draw pictures of the monsters then she would stamp on the pictures and tear them up.

If Matty died end Janet so Janet Johnson kills children on paper paper children to placate the gods.

'I can't imagine what use you can make of this. I'm a very ordinary person.'

At lunch Janet was benevolent, smiling at the head of her table flanked by the two men. Having never before given an interview in her own home, at such indulgent length, she was now drunk with the urge to self-exposure. She could say anything and millions would bend their ears: more than ever read her books. Bill this is Simon Judd, my husband Bill. Call me Simon. Bill smiled, squeezed her shoulder in the kitchen. Well done. It's going well. Your wife's a perfect woman, Bill. I know. Perfect poulet au blanc, sauce not too thick, I say what a super wine.

'The beams were plastered in the most frightful cream paint. It took us months to strip.'

Matty off for his rest. Hug Matty. Bye-bye, love.

'All this . . . '

'Well, we like it, don't we darling.'

Window open, warm air, bee among the roses. Commuting, converting cottages, living in the country. Telly. Scandalous tales from Simon who is after all rather sweet. Certain lady author who tried to seduce him.

'Not *her*? But I thought . . . '

'Apparently not.'

'Coffee?'

'The most frightful things! They start all uptight about telly then they forget, poor dears, and out it all comes, the lot, you'd never believe. The yards of film we waste. I ought to be a priest, no?'

'Brandy?'

'But it's perfect here. I could stay here forever.'

'Of course writing is very lonely. However understanding your family are, you're on your own.' Janet Johnson, slightly tight, imagines sleeping with call-me-Simon who is paid to be absolutely riveted by every word she says. An illusion, of course, she knows, but she is disarmed. Janet Craig-Cooper accepts a kiss from her husband who is going to put the mower together again. Nice meeting you, see you later. Goodbye, Bill.

This is the crunch, formal interview face to face before watchbird camera which through lunch was hooded beneath a black cloth, now waits. Simon is male nurse, big brother, lover and priest. Very gentle. 'I'll just ask you a few dull questions and you say what you like. We can always cut. Smoke, drink, do a strip if you like. Just be yourself.' Who?

Some technical stuff about light meters and sound. Trouble about sibilance. Just say something.

'I'm terribly sorry, I can't think of anything to say.'

'OK, Stan?'

Thumbs up from Stan.

'All systems go.'

Intro from Simon, blah about talented young author, sixth novel, one of the best women novelists writing today, also wife and mother. Own life so clearly er-happy, er-content, striking contrast between author herself and the deeply disturbing questions she poses which challenge the foundations of our everyday lives. Janet?

Outside, through the double-glazing, Matty is trundling a wooden horse round the pond. Mrs Munnery will be washing up. Matty and Bill are discussing the mower like old men. The continuity man is reading Bill's *Yachting World*. The room is full of cables and heavy-breathing strangers, only Simon familiar, head cocked sympathetically for Janet Johnson.

'Can you tell us, perhaps, how you arrive at these themes? Is there an, er, conscious motivation on your part?'

'Fear. I am frightened all the time. When I was a child I was frightened of dogs.'

No more than a flicker of alarm on Simon's professional face. This was an easy job, a rather dull, sensible female who wrote reasonable books that were supposed to be terribly perceptive, his secretary said. A good cook too.

Pity. She's off again.

Smile for the camera. 'You see I'm frightened of death, of my husband dying, or Matty, or me dying. When I had Matty it took three days and I thought he was dead, I thought I was going to die and when I came home the colours were too bright I could only go out at night.

'Let me try and explain. You see you can't write about your own life exactly or it would just be like screaming so you change it about a bit and by the time you've finished and put all these people through these perfectly ghastly situations the problems have become theirs not yours.

'So then you're free to go through the whole process again, in fact you have to go on doing it because that's the only way you can forget what a mess you are yourself. I mean the critics have been terribly nice and they say how clever she is, creating this real world, contemporary problems, all that. But it's not a world at all, it's a bolt-hole.

'If I were honest I'd write a scream but I daren't. The truth is I don't care who else is mad or crippled so long as it's not me and I don't have to look. Writing isn't looking, it's running away.'

Drink, he had said, smoke, so she drinks and smokes. The camera is interested. It explores politely the implications of bottle and glass. Janet Craig-Cooper does not approve of Janet Johnson. Janet Johnson is tight and she may be a bitch.

'My husband? Is an angel who doesn't know I've killed him, the walking dead. He's someone in a story I made up and I can't live without him. I was dead and he came with me.'

There was an electricity cut so they did not see the programme, which was a pity since it made good telly and sold a lot of books. They read aloud by candlelight and held hands, because they were deeply in love, so far as love is possible. And they lived together after that for a long time, until they were dead.

1972

10

Figments

'Who is that woman in blue, on the beach? And the girl?'
'That is Sandie Outram with her ghost daughter.'

Every morning Ms Sandie Outram, the novelist and person,
wakes early in her beach-house, rises clear-eyed and switches
on her electric kitchen. Though she is a good waker, the light
from the sea is too bright before ten so she does not open the
blind and the sun is received through slats. Wearing caftan
and towelling mules, she plugs in the coffee-pot, the liqui-
diser, the toaster, the air-conditioner, the waste-disposal unit
to gobble up last night's detritus, which is fishy, this being the
seaside. Her kitchen hums. Pug-pug says the coffee pot. Soon
Ms Outram will switch on the filter that cleanses every day
the little blue pool, hardly bigger than a tear among the chain
of pools that are preferred, on this coast, to the sea.

She flicks on the radio and cannot be doing with hijacking
of jumbo jet by Japanese terrorists before ten o'clock. Radio
off, television on without sound. There is the big, fat plane
roasting on the tarmac. She has noticed a hard line lately. It
will be stormed. Snipers already wait, probably, though God
knows where on that lunar landscape.

Her own breakfast finished, Ms Outram lays a pretty tray,
with toast and orange juice and milky coffee. At the last
moment she adds a fuchsia head in a narrow liqueur glass
and Sandie Outram carries the tray out of the kitchen, down
a short corridor to a small white room. Sandie puts down the
tray at a certain angle on the cane side-table and says to her

76

ghost daughter: there has been some terrorism.

It will be a glorious day. I have decided that you prefer toast to brioches. You will wear the orange shift today, for the beach, though of course you will change for the party to-night. Or perhaps you will refuse to change and we will quarrel. I shall have to think about that.

The girl steps naked from the bed and walks around the room eating toast (she would have preferred brioches). She is thin and brown, her hair striped by the sun, a touching little backside but breasts, thinks Ms Outram, too heavy, much too knowing for such an innocent. Though perhaps that is right? Time will tell. Ms Outram has learned to trust her instinct.

The ghost daughter is always dreamy before ten, not ex-actly sullen. She opens the shutters and yawns at the sun. Really, Sandie thinks, smoothing the pillow and shaking the single duvet, she is very fond of the girl, quite devoted. On such a splendid day it would be good to give her a treat. Perhaps they won't quarrel. Maybe they will take a delicious picnic to the beach: crab and crisp salad and half a bottle of wine. But, of course, the daughter needs company of her own age, Sandie has been thinking about that; she has given it a lot of thought, not that the girl has ever complained.

She touches the ghost girl's breast, smiles, brushes cheeks, promises.

'Perhaps this is the day you will meet your daemon lover!'

Along this little strip of coast, in the rich beach-houses be-tween the scorched hinterland and the polluted ocean, Sandie Outram's ghost daughter has long been accepted. There was curiosity at first, of course, and there is still gossip. When Sandie sleeps, Marianne, the ghost girl, disappears, naturally, and the first time this happened in public at one of Muriel Crosby's duller dinner parties, there was comment. But waking, refreshed, as she always does, Sandie Outram carried it off. Whatever you say about Sandie, she has style. Besides, there is always some new scandal to distract, this summer as any summer. Herman Trailer and his second wife have axe fights on the beach most nights. Since April there have been two suicides, one breakdown, one vasectomy, a quite serious shark scare, several shoals of sea fish washed up polluted to death on the seashore, and Herman Trailer is said to have had carnal knowledge. That is probably flattery but it is true that Trailer leapt on Marianne behind a rock at a beach party, and might – given a fair wind – have penetrated had not Sandie Outram at that very moment, poised to write the rape of her ghost daughter by a world-famous boxing playwright, yawned and dozed off over her typewriter, leaving Trailer on the rocks.

Marianne, who was Marie until Mu Crosby said that sounded like an au pair, picks her way through the rock pools, as far as she can get from Sandie and Mu knocking back Bloody Marys up by Jake's beach-bar. Sandie's having trouble with chapter four and Marianne is accordingly enervated. It seems to her sometimes that she has no future; she looks into the still pool and sees no reflection: molluscs, albino spidercrabs, are better off. Even Trailer might have been better than nothing. How wearisome it is, Marianne thinks, to be the victim of a writer's block. She suspects (actually she peeked at the typescript) that Sandie is torn between the long-promised daemon lover and anorexia nervosa. Or perhaps first the one followed by the other. Neither option attracts Marianne who, given self-determination, would probably be a sweet, rather quiet girl, inconspicuously happy. Marianne with her toe sets all the tiny, urgent forms of life dashing around their murky pool and, round-shouldered, almost invisible, wonders if fisherboy-barman Jake has noticed her. No daemon lover he – though many old rich women would have him. But Jake for her? No, Mother Outram would never allow such simplicity. Life now, it seems, has sad endings.

There she is, calling Marianne to heel.

'Marianne, don't stay too long in the sun.'

Mu Crosby is Ms Sandie Outram's best friend. That is: they play bridge together, exchange recipes, gossip about other women and irritate each other in a companionable way. Everyone but Mu is a little in awe of Ms Sandie Outram. Mu Crosby is in awe of no one and, in the way of rich, healthy women, cares nothing for anyone's opinion. Unlike Sandie, she dresses expensively and badly and eats too much. Wearing pink stretch slacks, she sits now at Jake's beach-bar before a plate of fat pink prawns. Shellfish will probably kill Mu but not yet.

Mu says: 'The poor girl. I don't see why you can't give her a reflection. Sometimes I think you're quite brutal, Sandie.'

'You'll kill yourself one day with shellfish. A reflection's out of the question.'

Mu shrugs. 'Well, she's your daughter, Sandie. So to speak.'

'You know I'm quite devoted to her.'

'You've a strange way of showing it. Letting her drift like this – look, she's getting quite round-shouldered. I think, Sandie, a girl needs companions of her own age.'

Sandie frowns at the sun. 'I'm aware of that, Muriel. But I have a block.'

'Hard cheese.'

Sandie sighs. 'Writing is not tinning pilchards, Muriel. Sometimes I wish it were.' Not that Sandie will moan. She cannot be doing with moaning writers, with any of the self-regard that so often accompanies the creative act. If Sandie were a man, she would probably dress for work like a stock-broker. When he was alive she used to approve of T. S. Eliot because he had worked in a bank and once she met him posting a letter on Cheyne Walk just round the corner from his flat, and he did not look like a poet at all.

Muriel is saying: 'Jake for instance. He's a dear boy.'

Sandie, preparing to leave, drops into her tapestry hold-all, menthol cigarettes, lighter, Sylvia Plath, Mu's recipe for *taramasalata*, sun barrier-cream and fluoride toothpaste Jake has brought her from the drugstore in town (all you can buy by the ocean is beach balls, pizzas from Jake's take-away pizza bar, sun oil, sun hats, snorkels and slippers, postcards and the sort of shell jewellery Mu Crosby wears, which is her own business, but she gives it to people for Christmas; once Sandie did find among the rubbish one beautiful whalebone pendant which she may give to Marianne when she decides what to do with her).

The sporting crowd has taken over the beach. Some young Germans are playing a complicated ball game. The sun is high. Wearing singlet and trunks, Herman Trailer jogs along the fringe of the sea. It is a very beautiful, shimmering picture. Sandie shivers.

'A ghost walked over my grave.'

'Goose,' says Mu.

'Geese what?'

'Walk in graveyards. Though I can never see why the hell.'

Jake is preparing the barbecue for the Trailers' party this evening. Though he is too sweet ever to think so, it is Jake really who runs the beach. He has long blond seaweed locks and may love Marianne. That would be natural. But he is shy of her, sees her as something odd and unaccountable: a revenant. A fish who will slide, sad-eyed, through his fingers, slip the net, mermaid wife.

'No,' says Sandie Outram, firmly. 'No, Jake's a good boy but no daemon lover. Not at all.'

Ghosts. The light shifts. Dusk on the beach, no chains rattle or doors creak but Sandie Outram broods in her room above the ocean, smokes too much, accepts the Trailers' party as inevitable, for Marianne's sake, and thinks I am tired, I would like to be an ordinary woman, but I am writing a story. It seems to be a ghost story. Perhaps we are all haunted, one way or another. There are the fishing boats going out, hardly a fleet any more, they'll be out all night. I should wax my legs. This is a nice room on the beach. The window is black like a curtain, pierced by the little, fish-frying fires. Beyond the horizon one might tip over the edge of the known earth into darkness; or so it looks tonight – the fires as brave as beacons outstaring the deadly sea.

'Look!' calls Ms Outram to her ghost daughter. 'Look, aren't the fires pretty.' And they stand, the mother and the child, arm in arm, cheeks to the dark window, while one by one the barbecues are lit to announce the finest party of the season, down that coast.

'What do I look like tonight?' asks the ghost daughter wistfully, since mirrors do not serve her; though she can, if Sandie wills it, walk through walls.

'I think,' says Sandie, 'you can't make up your mind what to wear, you put on too much make-up, change half a dozen times, then at the last moment slip on the pale green and scrub your face. No jewellery – except perhaps this whale-bone pendant.'

'We quarrel?'

'Not tonight.' Sandie shades her eyes, though it's dusk and the lamps are discreet. 'I have a migraine coming, I think.'

Sandie does look tired and Marianne is sorry. The ghost girl's ties with her mother are stronger, after all, even than flesh and blood.

'Lie down. We don't have to go to the party.'

'You're a dear girl. I don't deserve you. I don't know how I ever thought of you. But we will go to the party. At your age you must have fun. And it will be good for my block.'

Where does Marianne go, Sandie wonders, when I am sleep-ing? We have had some good dreams together and a night-mare or two. But sometimes I don't dream or I dream of others and where does she wander then, poor ghost? And all my dream people? Mu said once when I asked her: to one of Herman Trailer's parties, where else? But that's how she talks, that's Mu.

The party of the season starts in the Trailers' beach-house which is not exactly a changing-room or even a studio like Sandie's, but a wonderful cantilevered structure poised in mid-air reaching out at different levels from the sheer rock so you could look up from the beach and see the beautiful people dancing apparently like angels on air. Though struc-turally it is perfectly sound. A pupil of Nervi says. And there was nothing Nervi did not know about cantilevers.

Mu Crosby in an unsuitable pants suit says I'm not dancing on fucking air. Where's all this fish food? Lead me to the lobsters.

Sandie yawns. 'Do shut up, Mu. Mimi Trailer looks doped. She usually is. D'you think she'll get out the axe tonight?'

'Not before din-dins I hope. Herman's got to cook that fish.'

Marianne comes up with a plate of *vol-au-vents*, looking very pretty in her mermaid green. She longs to ask if Sandie plans for Herman Trailer to be her daemon lover tonight, and hopes not.

'I thought I might help with the cooking on the beach?'

'Of course, if you'd like to,' says Sandie and Marianne bends down to kiss her cheek. I could keep her with me forever, thinks Sandie, my ghost daughter. But I'll have to let her go, I always do, how sad. The oncoming migraine confuses her. She wonders how many at the party are her phantasms: maybe she made it all up, summoned from the fruitful dark this coast, these people, this season? The one world nudges the other. Once a suicide she had dashed off carelessly telephoned in the middle of the night to say he'd thrown up the sleeping pills and was stuck in purgatory, which was rather like a wet Sunday in Wales – would she please settle the matter one way or the other. Gas was no good because he'd been converted, and he didn't fancy all those dreary Mishima freaks so seppuku was out. So Sandie blew him up with his own bomb in a Boeing in the paperback edition and got a nice postcard; airmail, of course.

Pull yourself together, Sandie Outram, this is not your style.

Mu cuts in. 'Off you go, dear girl. Leave the grub.'

At this point in the party there is a lot of kissing. My God, thinks Sandie as Herman Trailer nibbles her ear, I could never have invented you.

Herman sits at her feet, fifty-year-old ex-boxing playwright dressed as a boy. Makes much sexy play of the creativity he believes himself to have in common with Sandie.

'She's lovely,' he says, meaning Marianne. 'It'll be a great book. Can I have her?'

'Ah,' says Ms Outram, with the smile of an elegant crocodile. 'That's the point, Herman. Can you?'

'You bitch. Just because I've gone off-Broadway.'

'Oh, Herman, Herman,' says Sandie Outram taking his hands. 'I want the best for her, you see. A daemon lover.'

'You're a violent woman, Sandie Outram.'

'Break it up, you two,' says Mu Crosby. 'Come on, Trailer, fry that fish.'

At that last, best, party of the season, there are a number of realities, none of which is necessarily absolute.

For instance, Herman has asked some tiresome characters from his last play or they have gate-crashed; anyhow, axe-woman Mimi can't stand them and becomes terribly drunk railing against these ratty, spaced-out girls and pot-smoking faggots, as she so elegantly puts it before Herman hits her and she shrieks he is written out. Why doesn't he go off and screw that Outram woman's ghost daughter if he can. Which he does.

Or, Herman and Mimi Trailer are touchingly reconciled. He is naturally tempted by Marianne, but then suddenly weary of the chase, of all this young flesh from which he can borrow nothing. In an excess of tenderness he sees how time has smudged too Mimi's keenness and brightness. They have been too frantic. He takes her glass, whispers in her ear and they walk hand in hand by the sea.

(That version would have to be very well written to hold water.)

Then there is another version in which Mimi catches him behind a rock with Marianne and chops off his hand. Now Herman is the only known left-handed ex-boxing playwright off-Broadway. (In the out-of-town try-out Mimi posts the bloody hand to Trailer's agent but the mail service complains so this *grand guignol* coup is written out – anyhow there is nothing special about Herman Trailer's right hand nowadays, as Sandie Outram says, what with all these people being kidnapped and the post over-burdened with fingers and ears.)

The beach is soft and dark. There is a grace, now night has fallen, to this last party. Even the gate-crashers are hushed, someone is playing a guitar, Sandie and Herman, fellow soldiers, exchange wry salutes across the fire. Oh well, they mean, what a life: writing. Mu Crosby cracks a lobster claw. There's sand in the crab.

Marianne says to Jake the beach-boy as they explore each other's salty bodies, 'I do hope she doesn't fall asleep.'

'You're not quite solid.'

'Hush,' she says. 'My mother might see.'

'I could put my hand right through you.'

'But I'm fond of her.'

'All we have to do,' says Jake, 'is go and tell her. We're not playing her games any more.'

'She means no harm. She wants the best for me.'

'Is Herman Trailer your daemon lover?' Jake's suddenly furious.

'Do you believe in ghosts?' she says. 'You must believe in me.'

In one draft Marianne and Jake go off together and live happily ever after in an abandoned coast-guard station, even out of season. For a while anyway. He gets used to it in time: her being a ghost and the way she can walk through walls. They are quite cosy, almost bourgeois, and after a few years Marianne, Sandie Outram's ghost daughter, puts on weight and no longer disappears though she is quite ill the night Sandie Outram dies.

Alternatively, Marianne is raped by Herman Trailer, out at sea in his Chris Craft, and washed up in the shape of a lobster Mu Crosby eats. Mu dies screaming of crustaceans and hauntings and phantasms, but then Jean-Paul Sartre believed, after he had taken some drug with empirical intent, that he was followed by lobsters and he got over it, and he's as sane as anyone now.

The only thing that is certain is that this was the last party of all on that coast. Afterwards there was the salmonella, and the pools were drained, then everyone went away. Christmas cards were exchanged for a few years but the beach-houses were empty. The sea was declared officially poisoned, on the beach a rash scavenger might pick his way between the coke tins, the French letters, the tar, the detergent, the ruins of the holiday.

Flotsam and Jetsam (murmured Ms Sandie Outram the novelist, returned for the sake of old times) played the music halls for many years and some summer seasons.

There's a dead cormorant. Silly bird.

Sandie made the sun to set and shivered, though not with cold. Sat in her car, decided not to smoke, wished Jake's bar had not closed down, missed Marianne. Even Mu.

She put out the lights round the coast, one by one, dowsed the moon, and consigned the world to darkness.

Then she drove off, though there was nowhere to go, no one to meet on the road, no road.

1978

11

Trystings

Rheims, 1250

From Henri De Millechamps, scholar and high cleric, given to the flames for the heresy of Pantheism, because he believed that God was in all things.

To his wife, Henriette, who at her husband's death, of her own choosing and with his accord, will take the veil of a silent order.

Listen, my love, for I shall tell you a wonder. A consolation and a joke. They roast me tomorrow for Pantheism when Animism is my crime. Though I do believe that God is here, in me, in the rats also that keep me company and in the straw of my pallet, the rose you slipped this morning through the grille – still, when they burn me they will set my soul free not to travel to God's judgement but to find another lodging upon this earth. As a bee, perhaps, or a prince or his whore, or as a footstool in your quiet cloisters. Even in you. Henri-in-Henriette-in-Henri, that is what I have sought through my long years of transmigration. Is my name not already in yours?

Can you believe this? That I have lived forever? Seeking you always through the streets and gardens of the years? Perfectibility, for me, not to reach some Orphic heavenly sphere but to join the half of my separated soul with yours, the other half. And then, perhaps at last, to lie as one in God's

86

bosom. Sometimes I think that you have glimpsed this. That you knew, the first time we met in this incarnation, that we were not entirely strangers. When you look up from your sewing or lie in my arms believing me asleep, and I catch a studying gaze of questioning, wonder. For you too, my dear, though you know it not, are a traveller.

Once, when you were a child in Egypt, I was a pebble in your hand. You let the warm sand trickle through your fingers and kept me for a day.

They have just brought in my candle and seem astonished by my composure. I actually laughed at the boy, who crossed himself and ran from the room, thinking me Lucifer crazed. Now I regret that I scared him, but it was all I could do not to shout after him, after all of them: Think on Bede! *Burn now your candle as long as ye will: it has naught to do with me, for my light cometh when the day breaketh!*

Now I am alone again and at this dusk time, when it is still sunlight out in the bright world, I confess to you, my last and one true confessor, that I have been weary sometimes of my long journeyings, my sinking and awakening, and hoped that the brief sleep between lives might be the last.

Shall I tell you the hardest pain for those of us who live forever and do not forget in that small darkness between incarnations? That is that though we may walk the streets as a man, solid, know man's ills and joys, die his seeming death, may love as I have loved you and laugh on a spring morning in good company — we, the *immortels*, feel ourselves to be shades, ghosts, revenants, visitors from eternity.

Do all return? I believe not. And of those who do, how shall even I, who have the knowledge of returning, know my brother-in-arms who fell with me at Marathon when next time he comes as a pig and I a butcher? Only you I always know, my love, even as a spider or a blade of grass.

It may be that I am the only one who remembers, of these wandering souls, these *vagantes*, passing from clay to flesh for the thousandth time, as though at first creation. It is a heavy knowledge.

They have brought me wine and bread and I spoke softly to the boy. Seeing me melancholy, he no longer fears me, and we talked for a while. Now he is gone, I think, this is another wonder: how we cling to life, even as a speck of dust trodden daily underfoot. Even I, at each death, whether terrible or seemingly composed – *in extremis* some Self has mewed like an infant to return. Even as they lay the pennies on my lids, or, as tomorrow, the flames leap to consume me, I wonder already: what next?

Now refreshed by wine and a walk around my cell, I ponder, my love, how, once you have dried your tears, you may frown and ask wifely questions. In answer I must truthfully admit that yes, I have been wed before and one of them was beautiful. But I was always in search of you and, failing to find you, have treated those women abominably. As a pander in Piraeus, I whipped my whore because she was not you. In England, as a countryman wed to a sweet and milky dairy maid by whom I had five children, I hanged myself in the barn and broke her heart. The Roman beauty left me for my foul temper and it was then I almost vowed to seek you no more. To grieve no more women, to assuage my thousand-year weariness, I ran a little mad from the court of the Caesars, took ship for Greece and beat my head against the Delphic rock to pray for a last death.

The romantic tales couples have told me of the one-to-be-loved glimpsed across a room, from a carriage or a window, and the brave pursuit! The fortunate meeting! After how many years or months or weeks! And I nod and smile (they think in congratulation) at the little flicker of their lives beside my long journey through eternity.

Immortality, I can tell you, does not bestow wisdom, nor grace. You have travelled as I have, but God has granted you the mercy of oblivion, so each time, as a babe in the cradle or a new-born cat, or a flower opening, or a butterfly bursting its chrysalis, you have woken forgetful and shriven.

Sometimes, in this my present disguise, I have sat with the dignitaries of our Church, solemn as puddings at Orléans or here at Rheims, Paris, Winchester, Oxford, Rome, Chartres, with William of Auvergne or Philip of Greve, and wagged my head when I wanted to howl with laughter that they were discoursing with an asp who suckled at the breast of Cleopatra. With the horse of Attila the Hun, a jewel in the crown of Charlemagne (where you too blazed, my dear, but you have forgotten). Imagine their faces, my dearest Riette, if they knew that tomorrow they are burning a flea from the middens of Nero's Rome!

But the candle gutters, you will be shivering for me in the first, false dawn. Later, I hope, I may think of you sitting, Henriette, so demure on your stool, with a coif like the wings of a bird and your eyes cast down, while you finger your rosary; and you will not be disconsolate, you might even smile and try to guess if I am that pretty little prayer bead. And you will not hasten to your death, too impatient for the next awakening, for who knows, in a universe and an eternity so vast, where we might meet as I do crave: not merely as husband and wife, but one body and one soul?

They have offered me a confessor, brought him in, all long face, distaste, and perfumed against the stink of my cell, but I have sent him away. Who but God could absolve the sins of a thousand years? They believe me intractable when I – who have advised you against impatience – long for the stake as a bridegroom for his wedding altar. They are merely freeing my soul to fly in search of you.

My hand is cramped, and that, at least, will be soon cured. Read these words, my wife, you must trust me, believe, re-member. When, as my friend, you send kindling so that the flames will mercifully lend me a quick consummation, you must remember everything I have to tell you, although it is a strange tale. Believe every word and die well, for that is my superstition – as you die, so may you be reborn. And the next time be on watch for me, your husband, everywhere – in men, in trees, in a bird at your window. In women too, for, as I must tell you, the spirit may pass even between the sexes. Do not tremble. There. Recall how our fingers touched this morning through the grille.

Listen. Watch for me. I kiss your eyes.

Hardly had the spirit leapt free than in Ethiopia the seed of a willow stirred. Full-grown, it gave shelter and shade to a bird for an hour or so. The bird flew off, the tree trembled. Axed, it fell quietly with a whisper and a rush. The sea, curling on a southern coast, lay back with each retreating wave to search that other ocean, the shoal of stars where she glittered, unknowing; burned out.

England, 1648

Testimony taken by the clerk, Richard Bewes.

My name is Henny Field and I am mumble-jumble. I scares children, for the wart on my nose and my poor clothes and my good black dog, my best boy, they runs from he and would hurt he if they can but he run faster. So we keep to ourselves and we are fine enough in our hut. In summertime the woods is pretty and my good dog might bring us rabbit and in winter he steal well though I am feared for him then.

I know the herbs and in secret there are goodwives who have come to me for curing their babes of phlegm or their own effusions of blood when the moon is too hungry for it, or for bringing on the blood when the moon is away and their times are stopped. Maidies too for prettying and for catching a husband-man, I have potions, but all from the woods and no harm. I will not make killing or hurting potions, although I am asked and they say that I do.

Magic too, they say, and bad witchery but I tell you, brother clerk with your writing, I have never done those bad things as taking milk from their cows or burning hay or making weather, so hail spoil their crops and thunder fright their children and turn the cream sour.

After they fetched me here they would have had my good dog too but I told he and he run off, though he would have in his head to stay. They say he be the devil and I take him to husband in my bed. But I am a virgin. Yet he does lie on my straw at Michaelmas cold for warming me. Is that a witch-thing I have done, clerk? To be brought to these questionings when I would be quiet with my Blackie? Henny is foolish but she knows enough thou make these writings for the witch-finder. Fear not topsy-turvy Henny, she hath no magic. If she had magic she would be home with her good dog.

Henny is wearied, Richard the clerk. They put her to the testings last forenoon and will again. Let me catch my breath, silly Henny. You look sad, brother Dickon long-face. Thee would not have this writing? See how pretty the sun is on your table. Smile. There. Henny can speak. No witch as th'm fool folk by thee say with their askings, only loopy-lally Henny Field. They can do their askings but Henny tell none but Dickon.

I no beauty never nor had power in the hair they taken, when they did the prickings too and the letting of blood and the one tooth in my head they pulled. The devil's teat's on my nose say Parson Rightly but 'tis not so, no devil nor imp suckles Henny's nose.

Matthew Woodman say I burn his barn by spells and would have me not for gallows but in the fire as they do in Scotland, nor will Parson Rightly stop him if he will. They've proven nothing on Henny but they'll have her, I know, by rope or water or fire. Not a'feared, Dickon clerk, not a'feared but for my Blackie if they catch he where he run. And that he be lonesome without Henny.

Do they bring thee to me now, Dickon? After water test and the Watching – day and night on the witch's stool – though no familiar come, nor imp, not even my poor Blackie, they break Henny's legs and must carry her to burning. So Richard the clerk must come to Henny's cell.

Did I sleep? The light goes and the boy is still here.

Listen. I will tell you secrets. Not witch's sorts but I have membrances, Dickon, dreams I had on the stool at the Watching when I slept and did not tell for they were puzzles.

I been wed, that is my secret. Though I be virgin I was wed, young and pretty on a spring morning. My dreams tell me. Then I forget. But bells remember me, big rolling bells in blue sky, and birds of a white dove I once had. And kissing and singing. Closer, Dickon, poor Henny's tired. And I speak in tongues that are not mine, in my dream. Mayhap I be a witch for I can say words. *Colombe. L'amour. La mort.* What would be those words?

Is that a tear, Dickon? Put that not in your writing.

'Tis but a little jump, like a bird from the window.

If thee can in secret, send kindling.

These be the last words of Henny Field.

Testament of the clerk, Richard Bewes.

Henny Field was burned for a witch this day, though burning is not the practice in England, this was done not by the Witchfinder but by her own people. I would they had not done this nor I stood witness.

Meaning to stay firm I stood upwind but still where she might see me. She went fast, thank God, and there was at the last moment a wonder, when a black dog, running too fast to be captured, leapt into the flames with Henny and was consumed.

Provence, 1960

Never would I have believed such happiness, that your soul, my darling, is in me. Friends pity my bachelor state and would marry me off – oh, the girls they used to put beside me tactfully at dinner and now the pretty widows! While I am more truly married than any man on earth.

Do you remember our childhood? The first time we knew – at seven, was it, or eight? – running on the beach and I first heard your voice in my head, laughing. You were angry when I didn't want to swim, you loved the water; you'd have drowned us, pushing my head under the water to see the bed of the ocean, the rocks, the reaching seaweed and that wonderful underwater light shaking gold. Were you a fish in one of your incarnations?

I have forgotten.

They called me a dreamy boy, they were cross, but how could I tell them I was listening to you? Are you sad today, Riette? Shall we drive down to the Corniche or the quay? You're not angry still about that woman in Italy? That American? I am flesh, you see, my darling but if I hurt you, I hurt myself.

I love you. Let's walk in the garden.

Just here, I thought perhaps a terrace? We could have a fig and train a vine on the trellis.

I was angry about the woman. I am the soul. I cannot close my eyes.

We are one, Riette.

Just so.

That's better. You're trying not to laugh.

Anyhow she had a fat bottom. What these women would say if they knew I was watching! But I would rather, I think, the other way round. Or hermaphrodite. What fun we could have then, Henry.

For a soul, you're very sexy.

Was I sexy before? Was I pretty?

To me always. And once a beauty.

Where was that?

Rheims. Our other marriage. Let's sit here. Look how milky the sea turns at night, it swallows all the colour of the day.

I remember . . .

Yes?

Blue sky, a dove, meat burning, flames. I am frightened of fire. Stay here quietly for a while. I'm frightened, I'm afraid of our death, to leave or be left.

This time will be the last, Riette. I feel it. Our separated souls have joined. This body is nothing, a husk. We shall leave it together. When I look in a mirror I see the eyes of a girl on a spring morning in Rheims. But we'll wait. We'll cultivate our vines. This is a good place to wait.

Provence, 1980

We are dying, my love. What a fuss they make.

Whisper or they'll hear us.

One now, truly –

It's darker.

Hurry! Catch my hand, run into the dark!

It will be lighter there.

1981

12

Hymeneal

Susan Edden, just married, comes to the farm in 1921. Up
the hill, but down in status, according to her mother, the
doctor's wife. She has spent her life on the edge of, but never
in farms. She comes up with Jesse ('Jesse', her mother says,
'sounds like a girl. Is that a name for a man?') in the cart, not
her father's car. Starting, she says, with a crispness that comes
naturally to her, as she means to go on. But really because she
fancies it.

Even outside the church, the two families keep to themselves. Eddens stiff and sweating in tight best suits; Aitkens
moving easily in their clothes, capturing the vicar. Kisses,
handkerchiefs, tears, some Aitken confetti, then suddenly,
miraculously, from the Edden side great boughs and
branches of orange blossom and lilac, spread at their feet,
piled in the cart. Jesse swearing and blinking behind flowers.
Joe, father Edden, missing, then up the road comes a flower-
ing bush, swaying, almost a tree, all white. It seems a long
time coming. The light shakes. Then, shedding some flowers,
it is tumbled across their laps into the cart. And Joe colours
and winks, first one eye, then the other, and just as embar-
rassing remarks and damp farewells seem inevitable, he
thumps the mare, like a barmaid, on the backside, and she
shivers, farts and leads off.

Someone has stuck cow-parsley in the mare's harness and
hung two little bells on the reins. The white dusty blooms
tickle her ears. It is a light cart. She trots and the bells ring.
Between the village and the bare hill there is a natural avenue

of bushes and trees. They move under white hawthorn, between high green, on their throne of boughs. Susan leans against her husband's shoulder. He puts an arm round her, leaving one hand for the reins.

'It was a lovely idea,' she says, and when he seems not to understand: 'the flowers.' Inside her head her voice sounds artificial, patronising. She would like to swallow her words, but no harm is done. He seems wrapped in some dream of his own. He is a small, brown, slim man, his only weakness, it appears to her, a shyness at having snatched her from the arms of suitable young men. She must reassure him. She blesses, for once, her intelligence, which will find a way to convince him of her love, his own worth.

He grunts: 'They'll want a do.'

'Yes,' she says, 'of course. They'll expect it. For them.'

'And you. It would be right.'

'Oh, me. I don't care about things like that.'

'You're a funny one.' For the first time since they were married, half an hour ago, he really looks at her, puzzled and loving. 'You know what you're in for? What you've lost?' He touches her cheek.

She laughs, clear-throated, easy. So that's what bothers him.

'If you knew . . . how boring those people are. What you've saved me from.'

'Perhaps.'

'Hurry,' she says, 'hurry. I want to begin.' They are out of the avenue and there is the hill and the house. She wants to throw open the windows, bring in flowers. The horse stops trotting and plods. 'Make her go fast.' She is excited and wants to tease him. 'Or don't you whip mares?'

'Oh yes,' he says. 'They're all the same, beasts.'

She likes to see him so sure with the reins. Something her father could not do. She congratulates herself on her instinct in choosing this man. She wishes only that she could spark off the same excitement in him. He kisses her softly on the cheek and touches the mare with the whip. They trot up the hill, shedding flowers.

The yard is smaller than she remembers, the ugly black barn bigger. A skinny dog runs out and barks at them. He

95

swears gently and it retreats, after a moment's doubt, wagging and cursing, back to its place under the barn.

'No,' he says, 'the front door.'

They go through the side gate, stiff, never used, to the front of the house. He has to kick the hinge. Between the house and the hedge there is half an acre of freshly turned earth. He is proud of this and shy. She knows that she must look pleased, though it's hard to imagine, at this moment, what she might do with it. He points to the boundaries. He has spent every evening in the last months, from nine to eleven, digging.

'There! That's yours. Your garden.' Anxious: 'You like flowers? You said?'

'Yes,' she says, and kisses him. 'Thank you. I love it.' Love, lovely, seem the only words she can say today. They don't mean much. They have been rubbed flat of meaning. But he doesn't notice. He uses words as the nearest tools that come to hand, rough and ready. Some fresher for his simplicity. She tells herself, I must go carefully; show him but not spoil him. She talks about roses and they go in.

She serves the cold chicken, puts away clothes and arranges her books. She can see how she might make this house her own, in time, with tact. Her mother caught her packing the books and said: 'You'll have no time for them.' 'Then I'll make time.'

'Your reading,' he murmurs, touching their spines as if they held secrets. 'I can hardly read more than my name.'

'I'll teach you if you like.'

'If there's time. Yes. I'd like that.' He looks at her in wonder. 'You're a queen, you know.'

She smiles. She is entirely happy and convinced of the rightness of her choice. 'But you too. You can do things I know nothing about. I'll be a fool, I know, on a farm. You'll have to show me.'

'You'll learn.'

After they have drunk tea (she would have preferred coffee but the tea, after all, tastes right) they go up. There is no electricity here, or gas. She is enchanted by the low-roofed room and the oil lamps. She turns them down and waits in the dark. She thinks he will be shy. He smells of soap.

'You've shaved.'

'Yes.'

'Kiss me.'

They have kissed often. This is familiar. She likes it, would like to prolong it. She feels very powerful, able to please him.

'Don't stop.' He pauses, propped above her on one elbow. His voice is baffled, almost resentful.

'Why did you marry me?'

She refuses to take him seriously. 'Now . . . let me see.'

'Not my money or my looks.' He is still solemn, quite stern. 'Nor my reading. Was it a fancy?'

'Jesse! What do you think I am?'

'I think you're a clever young woman, who, if choice were hers, would maybe never marry. Not as clever as you think. And you'd not be as content alone as you'll imagine, in bad times.'

She is touched by his seriousness. 'We'll have no bad times. I know it. Or none we can't overcome.'

He seems not to have heard her.

'And you wanted to do something with yourself. You've got pride in yourself. But you didn't know what. Just that it had to be something the others don't do. You might have gone to one of those universities, been a teacher. But you fancied me.'

'That's a terrible thing to say!' She is near to tears. They are whispering as if in church. She had thought she held him, quiet and small, in the palm of her hand.

'No. For most that's what it comes down to, fancies. All I say is, Susan, don't build on me, not too much. That is, you can count on me always, I hope. But don't think I can be owt but myself.'

'I don't understand!'

'It doesn't matter. It was best said now.' He smiles and pulls her hands away from her eyes. Then he begins to laugh and romp like a young dog. He fools about, and kisses and tries to be gentle, but it still hurts, more than she could have believed possible. At once, he falls asleep. She lies awake, hurt and bewildered. He takes her once more in the night, without even opening his eyes. This time it is better. But her wedding night is not at all what she expected.

The next three days – a long weekend – are good. The farm is still small. It will grow in the next forty years, but now it is possible for Jesse to take a short holiday. Through the four-day honeymoon an Edden cousin and another man keep things going but avoid the house, averting their eyes as they follow their sloped shadows across the yard when, in the early morning, woken by unfamiliar farm noises, Susan appears at the window.

'There's Tam. I think I've shocked him.'

He plunges his head in the bowl, pokes soap out of his ears.

'Not Tam. He thinks you're Queen of England.'

'And you?'

'I'll show you what I think. Give me that towel.'

'I might and I might not.'

He lunges after her, blind with soap, groping. 'You're a skinny cat.'

She sidesteps. Wherever she goes, he follows, but slow, threatening and swearing, roaring. It's like having a blind bull on a chain. They are behaving like children. This is the best time they will have.

'Give.'

'Say I'm the Queen of England.'

'I'm boggered if I will.'

He pins her down at last and wipes his eyes on the sheet. These are silly, private jokes. Instinctively, from a sensibility with which she does not credit him, he gives her all the nonsense she wants, but does not know she wants. She may deny later, even to herself, that she has ever been so frivolous. She has gone into this marriage, she likes to think, with her eyes open, determined that it shall be good and lasting: she sees them as reasonable friends, teaching each other. He will learn to read, to listen to music (for which she feels he has a natural, if untutored ear); she to be a farmer's wife. Concerning the second project she is vague but optimistic. She has always been competent. As for his education, that will be a matter of tact and patience and love. Their marriage will be all the richer – out of the ordinary – for these mutual benefits. She brings a great if invisible dowry and has a brain clear enough and a temperament cool enough ('Susan is such a *sensible* girl') to bestow it without offence or patronage. This is how her mind runs. She prizes her mind more than her looks. On one subject she might admit she is a romantic – common sense.

In these four days – after that first, odd night – her sensible resolutions are blurred by happiness. She notices, on the fourth day, that he is restless. His hands on the fine tablecloth (her mother's present) look foolish and empty. He wants to get back to work.

'You're worried about the farm?'

'The lambing's started. Tam's no shepherd. We can't afford to lose them.'

'Shall we go and see?' She has noticed the pen in the sloping field behind the house, up in the corner, where the hedge makes a windbreak.

'You wouldn't mind?'

'I'd like to.'

'You're a good girl.'

'No. I'm just your wife. Besides – ' she adds, with something of her natural airs ' – I've never seen an animal born.'

'It might be best if you stayed.'

'No. I want to come. If I won't be in the way?'

'You,' he says, and touches her cheek, 'you.'

They walk up the hill hand in hand. Up here there is a wind and the stars seem to be running, racing, falling. The couple pause for breath and look up:

'It's fine,' he says.

'Yes. It's lovely. You know them?'

'No. Only the Plough.' He jabs his thumb where the stars seem windiest. 'And the Milky Way. Tam knows them. He's learned them from fishing.' She knows what he means but likes to imagine Tam, sturdier and blacker than his cousin, monosyllabic, drawing in his trawling net great shoals of stars. She doesn't mention this. It sounds like the fancy of a silly girl. She frowns, as if dazzled, and says, offhand:

'It's strange to think some of them are dead. We're seeing them but they're not really there. You can think of space but not time. At least you can, but separately. Not time in space.' Walking with her face tipped up she catches her ankle in a root. He holds her and they go up.

Tam has a lantern in the pen. A ewe lies on her side,

apparently dead, but as they watch, the stomach, grossly extended between four skinny legs, heaves and flutters. The green eye of the sheep, still open, seems to observe them. Tam nods:

'I was coming down. But by the time I found her she was near finished.'

'She's gone?'

'Aye.'

'When?' Jesse looks angry. For a second Susan thinks that he might strike Tam.

'Now. A minute. Two maybe.'

'Knife.'

Tam blinks. 'You're going to cut her?'

Jesse has already flung off his coat and is kneeling. He nicks the ewe's belly, then remembers Susan:

'You'd better go back to the house.'

'Can't I help?'

'It'll need feeding, if it lives, till we can find it a ewe. Warm some milk.'

But she stays. Tam holds the lantern and she watches the two men, heads bent. She feels a fool, useless, but is too interested to leave. Then she is appalled as the womb is revealed and Jesse plunges his hands deep in like a woman in dough and pulls out the bloody mess. It's foul and marvellous. He's smiling. She stuffs her knuckles in her mouth and staggers outside to be sick. When she has finished she stays hunched, her cheek against the prickly black grass.

'I told you, get back to the house.' His voice is rough. He keeps his soft face for the lamb. She follows him down the hill.

'How will you get another ewe to take it?'

'Find one with a dead lamb. Skin it. Put the skin on this 'un.'

She stumbles but his arms are full with the lamb. She feels absurdly lonely, excluded, and then is ashamed of herself. Her voice sounds high and artificial:

'You did it so quickly. You seemed to know just what to do.'

'I'd better, it's my job.'

'But I'd have no idea . . . '

'It's what you know. Nothing special. Like your reading.'

'But that seems so pointless. It doesn't do anything for anyone but myself. It doesn't save a life.'

'A life?' he says. 'Don't go romancing about it. It's only a beast. I'd kill it as quick for money.' But his face is slanted away from her, towards the sheep, now kicking in his arms. 'You little bogger then, you want to run?' He sets it down and it wobbles in a circle back to him. 'I'm not your mam.' He picks it up again and now they're back at the farm. He says they'll keep it indoors for the night. It's sickly but should live. The honeymoon is over.

She stays outside for a moment in the yard. The racing sky makes the barn topple. There is a scent of hay and salt. She looks up, breasting the waves of darkness, to the high corner of the field where the stars are low and in the pen the lantern glows, a single small outpost of humanity in a scene suddenly cold and by no means benign. She shivers and goes indoors to warm the milk.

1972

13

The Interior of Henry

When Delphine Drinkwater met Henry, I was fascinated to see how she would do him over. I mean this quite literally, for over the many years I had known Delphine, I had come to realise that she was a spiritual decorator who could not resist the temptation to convert, as one might convert a house, the men who fell into her hands. Like flies into her parlour, they tumbled into her pretty boutique in Davies Street. The process, unlike death in the sticky web, was almost painless. They hardly realised that while their flats or their houses were being done up, they themselves were being subtly and not unkindly redecorated to Delphine's specifications.

To be fair, she admitted that charity began at home. She had been her own first client. She had been born in Leicester of tenaciously semi-detached parents who had christened her Muriel.

'Can you imagine,' she said, 'what might have become of Muriel Drinkwater?'

'Vividly.'

'Well, you can see. She had to go.'

I could not decide whether to be flattered or insulted by Delphine's confession. Possibly, she respected me. More likely she had come to the conclusion, early on, that I was no competition and she might therefore confide in me. Man's best friend, that's me. In any case, I was too fascinated to care either way.

You had to admire her. At an age when other girls were falling in love and buying the wrong hats, Delphine Drinkwater devoted herself to the single-minded fabrication of Delphine Drinkwater. That is not to say she was prefabricated. She simply saw, with a clear-eyed simplicity, the parts of herself which should be developed and those to be suppressed. She went from provincial art school to the Royal College. This was where I first met her, and from then on, I watched, like the tortoise the hare, her inevitable progress through a smart London store to the boutique. It was only a matter of time, as any tortoise could see, until she took over. Meanwhile, she exchanged her contact lenses for a pair of formidable horn-rimmed spectacles, began to shop at Bazaar, took evening classes in cookery, and disposed of her virginity as calmly and competently as she would have got rid of anything else in her life which seemed out of date.

The only way in which she differed from the fabled hare was, you could see from the start, that she was bound to win. She was perfectly honest about this.

'You see,' she once said to me, 'I believe that most people live in a muddle. I don't. I know what I want. It's as simple as that.'

'You're lucky.'

'Oh, I don't know.' She lit a menthol cigarette in a filtered holder. One thing she wanted not to do was to die before she had got what she wanted, whatever that was. So she took sensible precautions. 'I think,' she went on, 'it's metabolic. It depends if you are a burner or a storer of energy. I'm a storer.'

I had a few privileges. One was the right to tease her. That night she seemed expansive, so I took a risk.

'But don't you realise, Delphine, you simply can't treat people like this.'

'I don't see why not. Most men are hopeless. I show them how they ought to live.'

I knew what she meant. Under the influence of Delphine, George had gone off to Africa to shoot crocodiles. She had done up his flat as a hunter's pad, so obviously he must bring back a dead crocodile to complete the decor. That he was bitten by a peculiarly nasty fly and lost a leg was neither here nor there.

'You mean, how *you* think they ought to live.'

'Isn't that the same thing?' There was something sublime about such arrogance; sublime and fearful, so that, in that moment, I feared for Delphine.

There were no omens in the sky, no blazing meteors, nor did the dead rise keening from the grave, the day I introduced Henry to Delphine. If I am ever judged for this, I shall say that I had nothing more in mind than the convenience of both parties. Henry wanted his flat done up. Delphine did up flats. It was as simple as that. Henry wanted to spend his money. Delphine was prepared to take it. I was doing them both a kindness.

Henry rarely spoke above a whisper. Sitting in the Blue Pussy Club sucking an orange squash, he croaked: 'I need your advice, old girl.'

Wildly, I asked if he had got a girl into trouble and wanted an abortionist. He looked shocked.

'Nothing like that. I just can't decide between cream and white.'

I could have told him; Delphine simply did not acknowledge cream.

'All I ask,' she said, 'is a free hand. A completely free hand.'

'Of course.' Henry goggled at her sharkskin trouser-suit. Everyone always goggled at Delphine.

'Then that's settled.' She allowed him to touch the tips of her fingers. The men who fell for Delphine were either wolves or rabbits. Henry was a rabbit. I trembled, thinking another good man was biting the dust.

'What's the matter with you?' she asked.

'Nothing. A rabbit walked over my grave.'

'Oh you,' she said, 'you're a nutter. Come on, let's eat.'

I followed her out on a wave of Jolie Madame. As we left, I raised my hand to Henry in a half-salute. He didn't see me. He was gazing, with glazed eyes, at the tips of his fingers.

It looked as though Henry would be a walk-over. He was the perfect client, which meant, from Delphine's point of view, he had not an idea in his head. His personality was apparently that of the furnished flat which until now he had occupied. His opinions, like his furniture, were dull and borrowed. He was predictable. I could have told you, without reference to Henry, what his opinion would be on capital punishment, law reform, Vietnam, pop art, nuclear warfare and decimal coinage.

You could not be beastly to Henry, because there was nothing there to be beastly to. Those who did try to provoke him from time to time found they were beating their heads against a solid wall of thin air. He was a vacuum waiting to be filled.

I said to Delphine: 'It's almost too easy. You can do anything with him. He's a sucker.'

She drew herself up to all of her five-foot-three and glared: 'You know that's not the way I work. Everyone has something about them.'

'Except Henry.'

She ignored me. 'I simply find out what it is and build on it. Look at Simon Shoesmith. And Jango.'

I looked at Simon Shoesmith and Jango and had to admit that she had done a wonderful job of psychological detection. What had they been before she got to work on them? Nonentities living in limbo; rich nonentities, of course. She had simply, and with immense patience, studied Simon until she discovered, buried beneath the man of property, the pillar of society, the company director, a would-be Brillat-Savarin. She had separated him from his dull little fiancée who didn't know the difference between *meunière* and Walewska, fired his cook, and converted the whole floor of his town house into a kitchen so splendid that Simon actually cried when he first saw it. In the process, she tore out half a dozen Adam fireplaces but, as Simon said, sobbing with joy into his *sauce Hollandaise*, what does it profit a man if he gain the whole world and lose his sole?

Jango was more difficult. Delphine suspected he might be creative, but having tried him on art, music and sculpture and had him fall asleep on her half a dozen times at the Festival Hall, she almost despaired. Then suddenly she realised that the spirituality she had suspected in him had its roots in something higher than art. He was an ascetic living in luxury, and only Delphine had the perception to see it. She made him let the whole of his house in Belgrave Square, except for one small room in the basement. She put bars on the windows, had the walls stripped to reveal the bare stone, added a few spots of artificial mildew (resisting the temptation to take out the damp course) and installed a trestle bed with a thin straw mattress. In these surroundings, he was merry as a monk and out of gratitude paid Delphine twice as much as if she had done up the whole house as a cathedral.

'But Henry,' I insisted. 'You've met your match in Henry. He has no secret soul.'

'There's something there,' she said. 'I know it. And I'll find out what it is if it's the last thing I do.'

To give Delphine due credit, she meant what she said. For all her ruthlessness, she was in a way both honest and oddly innocent. She really believed that everyone, even Henry, had something about them, some hidden virtue or genius, and until she had uncovered this, she would not produce so much as a roll of wallpaper. She believed in giving people not what they thought they wanted, nor even what they ought to want in fashionable terms, but what they really needed to be themselves in the deepest spiritual sense. I have said she was arrogant. But, the truth is, she was always right.

Henry, far from being a walk-over, strained her integrity to breaking point. While admiring her persistence, I felt sorry for Delphine for the first time. She neglected her other work. She turned down new clients. All through that winter and spring, I saw her or heard she had been seen with Henry almost daily. They were at the opera, the ballet, the theatre. They went to church, to political meetings, to the races. They were even seen at the zoo. But it seemed Henry was not an artist, a priest, a politician, a country gentleman, or a zoo-keeper.

'It's hopeless,' she sighed, and she had blue circles of exhaustion around her eyes. 'He simply hasn't got a vocation.'

'Why don't you just give him Chinese Chippendale and leave it at that?'

'If only I could. But I can't give up now. He's paying me, you see. He's very generous. And he counts on me. You see – ' she got up to go and I was shocked to notice she had a ladder in her stocking; Delphine was going to pieces ' – you don't understand Henry. He knows he's dull and he minds terribly. He's very sensitive.'

'Perhaps he'd do better with a psychiatrist.'

For a moment, I thought she was going to slap my face. But she burst into tears and ran away – to meet Henry, I supposed. Delphine was obsessed.

I once saw Henry alone, waiting for her in the Blue Pussy. If Delphine had gone to pieces, he appeared to be flourishing on their experiment.

'A marvellous girl,' he said, 'nothing's too much trouble for her.' I observed that his bottom was getting fat.

I was away for a couple of months, and when I got back, I had the feeling that Delphine was avoiding me. I saw her once or twice from a distance at the theatre and in a passing taxi, always with Henry, and I thought she looked positively drab.

We met once at a party and she said: 'I went to his mother's in the country for the weekend. It was hell. All that fresh air. I got walked on by dogs.'

'And you still won't give up?'

She shook her head and smiled, but faintly. She had lost her brilliance. 'I can't now. I've got involved. There's only one thing left to do.'

She stuck her chin in the air with something of her old defiance and turned away before I could argue. 'I'll have to marry him.'

It was a pretty wedding. Delphine looked brave and beautiful in a white crochet minidress, holding a single lily. When I kissed her, the tears dropped out of her eyes like oil. I wished then that I had smacked her bottom before it had been too late. We waved them off to Dolphin Square. They were to spend a couple of days in Henry's flat before flying off to Venice. I went out and got drunk.

I dreamed of Delphine in her white dress. She was getting married on a table in the Blue Pussy. Everyone was clapping. She threw me a white lily and said very clearly – although I knew somehow that the remark was for me and I was the only one who could hear it: 'It was the only way to find out.' Then I dreamed the telephone was ringing.

I woke up and the telephone was ringing. I looked at my clock and groaned. It was two in the morning. Henry's voice sounded brisk and businesslike, as if he always rang people up in the middle of the night.

'I say, old girl, I'd be most terribly glad if you could trot round.'

He seemed cheerful and quite calm when he opened the door. 'Very decent of you to come.'

In the sitting room, he offered me a drink, then with the air of a modest impresario flung open the bedroom door. I thought: 'Well, she was right. There's something about him after all. He's off his rocker.'

Not being an expert in these matters, I could not tell at once if she had been strangled or smothered. But I knew she was dead. My first thought before the horror to come was that she looked happy, triumphant, as she used to look when she had been congratulated by a satisfied client. She looked as if she had at last discovered the answer to a difficult question.

My second thought was: 'Well, he's found his vocation.'

1967

14

Body and Soul

'I could eat you.'

He picked up a small mound of her flesh and worried it like a dog.

'Grrr.'

'Down, Rover.'

She got up, stretched, and went to the bathroom. He lay there and wondered what he would have for lunch.

Everyone said they were made for each other. They met at a gala dinner for the opening of a new restaurant. He first saw her across the folded wings of a giant mousse done in the shape of a swan, the climax of the dinner in more ways than one.

Francis was a well-known gourmet. A writer on food in magazines. He never gave recipes, or only if you sent in a stamped addressed envelope. He wrote about the poetry, the soul of food.

Angela wrote too. Thin, highly successful novels. She had reached that rather pleasant point of fame where people had heard of her, but no one bothered her. She was left in peace to get on with her real love, cooking. She had a number of articles by Francis pinned up round her kitchen to inspire her. Sometimes she had friends for dinner. But best of all, she liked to cook for herself. When she was not writing she would spend a whole day planning and cooking a dinner which she would then eat alone. Truffaut was rumoured to be interested in making a film of her latest novel, about a man who murdered babies.

Physically they might both have been designed from the same prototype, male and female versions. Both were cheerfully fat, though not repulsively so, both had slightly protuberant eyes and pretty feet. They were so alike they were often mistaken for brother and sister, an illusion they encouraged for the spicy garnish of incest it added to their relationship.

After their first meeting they saw each other almost every day. Angela discovered that Francis was the only person in the world, besides herself, she really enjoyed cooking for. Francis found that Angela's was the only cooking, apart from his own, he really enjoyed eating.

These shared dinners in Angela's flat in Upper Cheyne Row were, in a way, their first love-making. For a while they needed no other intercourse than that of the mutually titillated and finally satisfied stomach.

Then one night, stimulated by a peculiarly subtle soufflé and a disarming little cheese, Francis went on to the fifth course, which was Angela.

'Darling.'

'You're delicious.'

'Mmm.'

A little later:

'What are you thinking?'

'That was a marvellous soufflé.'

'Yes, it was rather, wasn't it.'

'But this is better.'

It was the highest compliment he could have paid her.

Another thing they had in common was that both had been virgins. But they fitted together so well, that everything went perfectly from the beginning.

Yet they were, after all, two people with secret inner lives of their own, capable of surprising each other. While in one sense they became a single person, separated only by the few hours for which they must be apart, in another way, released by pleasure from the prison of shyness that had held them both, each discovered an unexpected identity. Voyaging together and yet separately, they looked down from the high point of happiness and saw revealed some previously unsuspected attitudes.

One night for instance, Angela laughed.

'What's funny?'

'Well, it's absurd isn't it? Sex and eating. If we could see ourselves. Guzzle, guzzle. Thump, thump. Such a fuss about a few carbohydrates and a spasm of the nervous system.'

Francis was a little shocked. He went home earlier than usual and tried to think of something new to do with duck. But nothing came. So he boiled an egg then found he had run out of salt. So he had a cup of coffee and went out. For the first time he really looked at women and girls. None of them came up to Angela. They were all too thin. He went home to bed and dreamed that Angela had been served up to him on a silver plate, steaming hot and garnished with parsley, with a peach in her mouth. When he put the fork into her she giggled.

As each became aware of a distinct, not very comfortable identity, Francis and Angela found they could not do without each other. Their love raised questions which could only be smothered by more love.

So, to ensure the continued presence of the other, they decided to get married.

They discussed the honeymoon.

'We could eat our way through France?'

But Angela was carsick.

Spain was out because of the food. Greece was too far because they had only a fortnight. So it had to be Italy. Angela said everyone was going to the Argentario this year.

'Well if everyone's going we'd better avoid it.'

'I don't mean *everyone*. I mean Jeremy went in May and Pen went last year and said it was so marvellous she stayed on and sold rugs till October.'

'All right.'

'Darling! I promise you'll love it.'

Angela was inclined to get her own way. She never sulked or fussed or nagged. It was simply that Francis liked giving her things.

Their relationship at this point in time was very finely balanced. The question of *celui qui baise et celui qui tend la joue* had not yet been settled. After all, they had plenty of time.

They flew to Pisa then got a train to Santo Stefano and a

boat to the island of Giglio. Pen had given them the address of a marvellous vine-draped, sun-baked *pensione* looking on to the harbour. They arrived in time for dinner on the terrace. Francis shaved and Angela took a shower. Her drip-dry Dacron dress was laid out ready on the bed. It was really a maternity dress. She had found that in her size the only smart designs were to be found in the stork department.

She stood under the shower and watched the water run down her big marble body. On the journey her ankles had swollen.

'After the holiday I'm going to slim.'

'Why?' Francis blew the stubble out of his electric razor into the wash-basin. Really he ought to shave three times a day.

'For you. I want to be thin for you.'

'But I love you as you are.' Francis was appalled by the thought of a thin Angela. He would have liked to stuff her with food till she grew even fatter. Secretly he was fascinated by the idea of the ortolan, which is kept in a box and stuffed to death till it is eaten. Not that he wanted Angela to die. Far from it. He wanted to say: grow fat and live. He had great hopes of Italian pasta.

'Do you really?' Stepping out of the shower with a towel round her waist, she was suddenly, touchingly, clumsy, wistful.

'Really.'

He showed her how much. They missed dinner that night. About one o'clock they woke up hungry. They shared a bar of chocolate, exactly half and half.

Francis was embarrassed to go down to breakfast. He felt everyone would have seen them arrive the night before and guessed why they did not come down to dinner. He wanted to sit inside at a dark corner table but Angela insisted they should eat on the terrace in the full glare of the morning sun. Francis felt as though he were walking out on to a stage. He nibbled a roll and drank two cups of black coffee while Angela worked her way through a bowl of fruit. Peaches, apricots, figs.

Angela sighed with satisfaction and tore at the purple flesh of the fig. The word that occurred to Francis was 'improper'. There was something indecent and exciting about the way

112

the fig gave itself to Angela's teeth.

You're turning into a sex maniac, he told himself. You see it everywhere. He had a recipe for a compôte of figs. He tried to remember it.

'You're turning into a sex maniac,' said Angela, 'the way you're looking at me.'

'Let's go to bed,' he said.

By the end of the first week they had re-established some kind of equilibrium. Whether it was a truce or a design for living, remained to be seen. Angela subdued the thin girl inside her trying to get out and obediently ate pasta once a day. The sensual glutton Francis was so alarmed to discover within himself, continued to make crude suggestions at inappropriate moments. Francis learned how to turn a deaf ear.

They had a few spells of radiant happiness when their impulses coincided: to eat a lobster, to make love, to do nothing. Then they believed they were the luckiest people on earth.

The harbour was like a stage set for a sugar-sweet opera, in which, after a few charming confusions, everything is resolved to the general satisfaction. Exit stage left, the villain confounded; exit stage right, handsome young fisherman and mayor's daughter, lovers reunited, wreathed in flowers. Applause.

At the top of the hill, however, was a setting for a different drama. An old fortress town which looked from a distance like an outcrop of rock and had an atmosphere of its own, altogether more sinister. Rossini had lived there and a delightful plaque on the church wall suggested that he would play the last trump in Heaven. But that was neither here nor there.

'It gives me the creeps,' said Angela. 'Even the people are different.' The fishermen down below were small, squat, dark and cheerful. Up here they were tall men, proud and serious hunters.

'They seem to look *over* you,' Angela complained.

'Why shouldn't they?' said Francis. 'We're only trippers.' He stamped through the narrow streets with his bottom lip stuck out, humming soundlessly. He seemed, implicitly, to have made up his mind that there was nothing special about the place. A dark-robed priest suddenly slid round the corner past them as though he were on rollers. Avoiding him, Angela and Francis were crushed together. They glared at each other. It was their first quarrel.

'Let's have a drink and some sardines,' said Francis.

Angela glowered. 'Food and drink. That's all you ever think about. And one other thing.'

'And why not? What else is there?' Francis was being purposely obtuse. He knew exactly what he was doing but he could not stop himself.

But he had not bargained for the effect on Angela.

She punched him in the stomach, stood for a moment paralysed by shock, then howled, covered her face with her hands and blundered off down the hill. In the harsh eye of the mid-afternoon sun she looked like some great white fowl, last survivor of an extinct race, which has lost the power of flight and must carry its heavy body, its impotent wings, the knowledge of its certain death, to the world's end.

Francis, winded, gave a slight groan, shrugged, and turning into the café ordered a half bottle of wine and a *fritto misto* of octopus and various small, unidentifiable fish.

Their honeymoon was at an end. They had discovered each other's weaknesses. Only one question now remained. What use would they make of this knowledge?

Later they patched it up. In the traditional way.

'My big bear.'

'My big white whale.'

'Tummy or bed?'

'Tummy then bed.'

Shellfish are said to be aphrodisiac, in which case they should have been perfectly suited to their programme. As it was, at the most inappropriate moment, Angela's stomach, curdled by drama and heat, rejected her dinner. Francis heard her flush away their warm intentions back to the sea whence they had come, and was moved by pity. All the more so when Angela, white and shaking, crept back to bed. They were very sorry for each other.

'Poor bear.'

'Poor whale.'

They kissed, like two nuns, and fell asleep.

In this mood they went home, a couple of invalids leaning together for strength. They were very considerate of each other. Francis made Angela drink mineral water for her stomach. In Pisa, Angela said Francis must have a proper meal and ate a pear with downcast eyes while he worked his way through the menu. In the plane they held hands and pretended they were happy.

They tried to please each other. Angela ate more than she wanted, Francis, less. At night, Francis, devoured by lust and hunger, would lie staring at the ceiling till at last he crept from the bed and, assuaging one appetite, pacified the other, with a leg of chicken from the refrigerator. Where once he had been a gourmet, now he was a glutton. While he was downstairs Angela took a stomach powder. She suffered from indigestion. In the dark she imagined her body, grossly distended; she dreamed that she was crushed under great mountains of food, that Francis was feeding her through her ears, her eyes, her nostrils. She screamed.

'Wake up, you're dreaming.'

They kissed and lay back to back, pretending to sleep.

Once they had been like twins. Now, if such a thing were possible, you might have said that a mystical separation had taken place. Francis was becoming the body, Angela the soul. Which in marriage is not a practical division.

Increasingly, body and soul clashed in open war.

Angela sat on the bed smoking and watching Francis undress.

'You're too fat. You're like a woman. You have breasts like a woman.'

'And you're too thin. You look like a boy. Soon you'll have no breasts at all.' It was true she was losing weight.

Even reconciliations were spoiled:

'I do love you.'

'So do I.' Both spoke the truth.

'Let's go to bed.'

'I'm not tired.'

'You're never tired. Till you get to bed. Then you go straight to sleep.'

'That's what bed is for.'

Francis groaned and put his head in his hands. He made

115

one last attempt.

'Come on.'

'It's so silly. It makes me laugh.'

He touched her. She giggled. She started to take sleeping pills.

They loved each other and yet they could not stand the sight of each other. For Francis, marriage had released the fantasies of grossness, dreams of the ortolan. For Angela it had exposed the monstrous and fleshy underside of appetites she had once regarded as altogether natural. In Francis she saw herself, as she might have been.

But because they loved each other they had moments of painful, temporary reconciliation. Beneath a flag of truce there were dialogues of tenderness. On such an occasion, they got a child.

Francis was delighted. This, of course, was the answer. Babies were good for women, they settled them. After the first three months, when she grew even thinner, she began to put on weight and by the fifth month had reached dimensions even Francis, in his wildest dreams, could not have hoped for. The effect on Angela was remarkable. The fatter she grew, the more she glowed, like a lioness, not with pride, but rage. Above her swollen body her eyes blazed, and she explained to Francis:

'I do want the baby, really. If I could find him under a gooseberry bush.' Francis tried to understand.

'It's this I can't bear.' She pointed at her stomach.

Francis thought to himself, I don't care so much about the baby, it's the tummy I love. But he had the sense not to say it.

He was afraid that she might hurt herself. He hid her sleeping pills. When she ate, as she did nowadays with a bitter and gigantic appetite, he kept his pleasure to himself. He cooked as he had never cooked before and thought of all that fragrant food turning to flesh.

The baby was a fortnight late. He realised that while Angela, as is the way of nature, after the seventh month had mysteriously submitted to her burden, he now dreaded the child whose arrival would leave her body slack and empty.

The evening before it began to arrive he cooked his best dinner ever. Just as he was clearing the table, Angela groaned and clutched her stomach.

She was three days in labour. Finally the child, a son as she had predicted, was born. And taking its first breath of life, killed its mother.

'A fine boy,' said the matron, 'nine pounds two ounces.'

Francis looked at the child asleep in its cot, its fat fists clenched in a boxing position. It was plump and healthy and Francis felt nothing. He could not even think, my son. If it had been smaller, Angela might have lived.

Francis was allowed to see the body of his wife.

Relieved of her burden she seemed quite thin, as if the flesh of those nine months had melted, and oddly peaceful. Left alone with her in the white room he could neither weep nor pray. He touched her lips with his finger, as though hoping for a message. He had really loved her.

1967

15

A Friend of the Family

'He stands on his head.'
   'Well almost.'
   'Come on Henry stand on your head.'
   'And dies for the Liberals.'
   'Die Henry.'
   'He can't do both at once. Don't be silly how can he do both.'
   'And dances. He really does dance.'
   'He likes dancing best.'
   'He got drunk once.'
   'Really drunk.'
   'We nearly died.'
   'Henry likes a drinky.'
   'Only vodka.'
   'He's a scream.'
   'What about a little drinky?'
   'Gorgeous.'
   'Heaven you could come.'
   'Bliss.'
That was Pru and Tim the first time I went to see them at the Hut. The Hut was where they went at weekends at Saffron Moulding in Sussex and Henry was their dog. He was a Basset hound and he really did do tricks. He was a proper clown. That was his only asset. Secretly, I never liked him much and when I got him alone I used to snap orders at him till he could hardly stand. Once I had him dying for the Liberals for half an hour. Every time he tried to stand up I

118

had him down again on his back. I don't think he liked me much either but he could never resist an order.

I am a bachelor. At the time I met Pru and Tim at Jenny's party, about a year ago, I had been studying for a long time to be a bachelor. It was a condition, I felt, to which I had been called. I had, to myself, taken vows.

Not because there is anything the matter with me, that you could pin down. I tried once to explain to a social worker I met in a train:

'It is like being in an aeroplane if you have ever been in one. You have a feeling of being disassociated. A lot of novels and short stories have been written about it, if you have read any of them. I send all my washing to the laundry, I have a good job and so I can afford it. I eat a lot of frozen food. I go once a week to an expensive restaurant. I do my shopping on Saturday mornings in a supermarket, except for meat which is sent by post from Scotland. I think sometimes that it would be nice to be like other people but that is pure sentiment. I cannot imagine what it is to be like other people.'

This makes me sound like a case which I am not. Perhaps I exaggerated a bit for the social worker. She gave me her address in case I ever needed it. In fact there are a lot of people like me but you don't notice them. We are inclined to efface ourselves, which makes it extraordinary that Pru and Tim ever noticed me.

It was Tim actually. It was a very hot evening and Jenny's party was giving me a headache when Tim came up and said:

'Hot.'

'Yes.'

'Timothy Creek.'

'Charles Harmish.'

'Advertising.'

'Publishing.'

Nobody wasted words in that weather. Except some of the women who couldn't stop themselves.

'Wife,' he said, jabbing a finger across his glass at a big girl with a wide open face and too much lipstick. But she looked nice. 'Pru. Are you . . . ?'

'No. You know.' I had found if I said that, people understood, or pretended to understand that I had somehow never

119

got round to a wife. Too busy or something. Tim nodded with solemn interested comprehension. I took to him a lot, immediately, and then Pru came up and we all smiled at each other and raised our glasses in a sort of toast. In a minute Pru tugged at Tim's elbow.

'Sweetie we must get back to Henry. He'll be in a state.'

'Child?' I felt the faintest pang of jealousy and disappointment. I have nothing against children but I have found that people who have them are a dead loss. Their eyes glaze over and even when they've left them behind they always seem to be listening for something.

'Dog,' Pru said and I was relieved.

There was a pause and I think we all had the feeling that we didn't want to separate.

'I know,' said Pru, 'why don't you come down to the Hut tomorrow? We've got a hut at Saffron Moulding. If it's very hot. If you'd like to.' Tim nodded as if he really wanted me to, so I said yes and in the end after we had all had spaghetti at their flat and collected my pyjamas, I went down with them to Sussex that night. They opened the top of the convertible so that the wind pinned back Henry's ears making him look almost intelligent. I found it very bracing, and exhilarated by the suddenness of it all, and this pleasant companionship in the face of the wind, wondered if I hadn't been alone too much. When we got there Pru made the beds, while Tim turned on the Calor gas and put a kettle on, I drew some water from the well. Pumping the handle up and down in my shirtsleeves, with the well full of stars from a blazing sky and the light of an oil lamp in the cottage window, my friends waiting for me indoors, I felt dizzy with a new-found love.

It got quite soon that we did almost everything together, so that people thought about us as Pru-and-Tim-and-Charles, sometimes as Pru-and-Tim-and-Charles-and-Henry – those who, unlike me, considered Henry rather sweet.

Every weekend we went to the Hut, and I had dinner with them regularly twice a week in London. Quite without coyness or any of that patronising female nonsense, Pru took over my chores, washing the woollens I did not care to send to the laundry, sewing on buttons (not darning my socks –

like most bachelors I had discovered the miracle of synthetics). She simply said: 'While I'm doing our things, I might just as well do yours.'

I can't describe the peace and delight of those first few months with Pru-and-Tim, but I shall probably try. Every Tuesday and Thursday I would leave the office in Bloomsbury, get a 19 bus to World's End, turn left towards the river, walk a hundred yards to the Victorian block on the Embankment where they had the top floor. I rang the bell, spoke my name into a little grille above the letter box (or more often Pru would speak first, saying my name with a question mark, and I would say Yes). Then the door would swing open and I would climb the twenty-nine stairs to their flat.

The flat consisted really of one room. You went in through a little lobby, with a bathroom leading off, into the studio where they lived and ate and slept. The kitchen was in a gallery and the flat had been photographed for one of the weekend supplements as an example of successful one-room living. There was a picture of it with Pru cooking in the gallery, chopped off at the waist, which I thought was a pity, and Tim adjusting the hi-fi. There was a blur in one corner, which was Henry trying to bite the camera but you wouldn't have known.

Pru was usually in the gallery doing something about supper, wearing a blue-striped butcher's apron and humming to the hi-fi.

'Charles,' she would say, as if she hadn't been expecting me and I was a wonderful surprise. When she smiled she put everything down and concentrated not just with her mouth but with her astonishing headlamp eyes. If you had been wanting to learn to smile you couldn't do better than go to Pru for lessons. After the first visits it was understood that I would go straight to the bar they kept in a nineteenth-century commode, pour myself a drink and talk to Pru while she cooked till Tim came in. When Tim arrived there would be a bit of a confusion for a minute or two, with Henry creating the traditional dog sort of fuss about the master coming home, then Tim clipped him on the ear with the newspaper, which shut Henry up and made him fawn obscenely. He was

an unexpected dog for Pru-and-Tim, by nature suburban.
He would have liked to fetch and carry things for Tim, like
slippers, but Tim never wore them.

'Well and how about Benchcramp?' Tim would ask, having
blown a kiss to Pru in the gallery and saluted me. Benchcramp was my own small contribution, apart from flowers
and the odd bottle of wine, to our sociability. He was my boss
and he might have raised his eyebrows at some of the stories I
told about him. Basically all were true, in that given certain
circumstances, Benchcramp would definitely have behaved
as I described. I had a tale a day to tell of his wild and wilful
behaviour and Pru-and-Tim never seemed to tire of him.

Dinner was eaten in the dining corner under a real oil
lamp, at first in silence – there was a certain sanctity about
Pru's cooking – then as we came to the cheese and fruit and
the room retreated before the advancing night, we sat like
enchanted moths in the lamp's benevolence and talked, in
low voices. We would have made a pretty picture from the
river, if you had happened to look up, a family or close
friends you would have imagined, and envied our harmony,
perhaps.

I cannot say precisely when a crack appeared in our
heavenly triangle. You would have thought us so close that
we seemed joined by the flesh, by a common birth, or a
painless grafting. You were aware of this when we were in a
room with other people, though at a distance from one
another, one of us alone seemed always to be bearing in mind
the other two. They said, those who had been friends of Pru-
and-Tim and now turned spiteful, that we took one another
to the lavatory, but there was not a grain of truth in this or
any of the other, less silly but more vicious suggestions that
we were indecently mixed up in anything more than a perfect
friendship.

It was, I suppose, my fault. Accustomed for so long to a
meagre diet, this banquet made me gross. I discovered in
myself an appetite disastrously outsize. Having once put up
with nothing, now I could not have enough.

It was about Christmas that the longings in my head took
on the quality of a positive pain. That is not an image, they
really hurt so that I even had my eyes tested. Keeping them

to myself was the worst thing – when for so long now I had been licensed to utter to kindly ears my smallest thought – but how could I say to Pru that everything she had given me, the food and sympathy, was not enough, what in the world could I expect of Tim that he had not already done for me? I succeeded only in worrying them, for they guessed something was wrong, we had grown so close, so sensitive to one another's problems that the slightest trouble, from a constipation to an injustice performed upon one of our members by an outsider, belonged to all three. We were closer even than a family, for we had chosen one another.

'Drinky,' said Pru when I came in from work, settling me down in a chair and shaking the snow off my coat. 'Drinky and telly.' When she had sat me down and put a drink in my hand she sat down herself opposite me in a rocking chair, an original bentwood Thonet she had picked up in Earls Court. She shooed Henry away who was hanging around hoping we would ask him to do a trick, or fetch something, and rocked, studying my face with such loving concern it was all I could do not to cry, to put into tears what I could not explain.

'Poor Charles,' she said, 'poor Charlie darling,' humming my name like a sort of incantation in time to her rocking, 'is it Benchcramp? Has Benchcramp been a beast? Has someone been horrid to Charles?' If they had, she seemed to say, she would kill them. 'Tell Pru.'

What should I have done? Gone away? Tried hopelessly to explain? Not, as I did, reached out for lovely rocking Pru and collected into my arms as much as I could grasp of her kindly, generous, consoling body. As we went down I caught a glimpse of Henry asking with stolid patience to be let out. He can burst, I thought, he can burst.

No, our friendship was not from that moment shattered, no, I did not immediately become guilty and resentful, Tim suspicious and Pru ashamed. Quite the opposite. Rather, things were better than they had ever been, better than I would have believed possible, all I had dreamed. Stupefied with turkey and wine, murmuring, sleeping, waking to nibble little nuts and mince pies, to play with our presents, we passed an enchanted Christmas, happy and bloated hermits in our high room, like lovers in a lighthouse. We were invulnerable, nothing could touch us, so strong we were with love.

Almost, I told Tim what had happened with Pru, so logical did it seem, so right and so little did I mind that we were forced to share her, that the two went off arm in arm each night while I slept alone on the sofa (where Pru joined me one afternoon when Tim went for a walk). That too seemed right, she and I together, as we had been now twice, and Pru-and-Tim as they had always been, but better perhaps, more fine, for what I had done. Jealousy, I thought, is not our business, it belongs down there in the street where we do not go.

When do you know you have eaten enough? How soon does the appetite sicken and die and the sated man turn like me from the table? I am sorry to go on about food but that is for me the image that recurs whenever I try to describe my one adventure in love and the way I gave it up.

'I think,' said Pru on the last night of Christmas, pouring coffee from the white Swedish pot I had given them for a present, 'that Charles might just as well stay. I think, why doesn't he just go back and pick up his things and let his flat and move in. I mean it seems so silly going back to that horrid little flat when he could stay here on the convertible.' She dropped a lump of sugar in Henry's mouth. His mouth was always open. I had always intended to put something horrible in it but now I shall never have the chance.

'Yes,' said Tim, with the serious, considering look he had when he liked an idea. I'm sure that was how he agreed with his boss at work. The frown and the slight pause added weight to his affirmative.

'Oh good,' said Pru, 'then that's settled.' She glanced round the room and I knew she was mentally rearranging the furniture to suit my convenience. 'Or we could put a proper bed in the gallery.'

Half an hour with Pru in bed before Tim came home from work. Every day if I wanted it. Helping Tim put up bookshelves. Walking Henry. Pru's good coffee for breakfast, hot croissants on Sundays. Coq au vin on birthdays. Lemon soufflé. The sweet scent of soft trout melting in almonds. Love every day. Always.

Perhaps for a certain type of person, like myself, the idea of love is always more desirable than the fact. Until this moment I had been a tourist, an enraptured visitor to love, who had imagined for a moment that he might like to stay forever in this wonderful land. But a visitor can always leave.

The suddenness and hardness of my decision was strange. Secret even to yourself, your mind comes to its own conclusions. Then someone, like Pru, asks a question, and up comes the answer, ready-made.

'No,' I said.

I only had my pyjamas and my toothbrush to pack in my briefcase. I said I would come back some time for the rubber plant they had given me for Christmas but I never intended to. I'd never have been able to look after it.

On the way home I bought some instant coffee for breakfast. What a stroke of luck I thought, the supermarket being open on Boxing Day.

1965

16

The Perfectionist

Of course the moment Jeremy saw Laura he had to have her.
I realise that now, but at the time it was Sophie, my wife – she
has an eye for that sort of thing – who noticed and told me. I
had never associated Jeremy with sex. I still have difficulty in
making this connection in my mind. Not because I had ever
heard anything to the contrary. It was simply that at some
point, for sex, you have to take off your clothes, and while I
can imagine most of my friends stripped for love I could not
picture Jeremy without his finely pressed suit, his silk socks,
his burgundy waistcoat, his Italian ties, and most of all, his
high-cut, soft suede boots. He could have kept his boots on, I
suppose, but while I have read about that sort of thing in
books I have never encountered it in life.

But I ought to have guessed when, at our party, Jeremy
pointed at Laura, fabulous in something sea green, and said
'Please', in the same voice he had asked for, and got, our best
piece of opaline, our Graham Sutherland (limited print series
number twelve), Sophie's secret recipe for *boeuf en daube*, and
my favourite rosé, Chapeau de Napoleon.

For Jeremy was a materialist, a collector. Not like the
indiscriminating magpie which will pick up anything that
catches the light, including the cheapest imitations, but like
Queen Mary. He never took so much that you could turn him
out of the house, but just enough to feather his nest, and only
the best quality.

And you could never refuse him. For you realised as he
stood with his head on one side examining your most

treasured possession, that here was a professional materialist, a man unlike yourself, to whom these things were more than a casual pleasure. They were as necessary to him as light and air, food and drink to the rest of us.

'You see,' he said when I talked to him about it once, when he was feeling expansive and friendly, having stolen a perfect housekeeper from his best friend, 'I am abominably affected by the slightest flaw. A crack in the ceiling can put me to bed, a chip in the base of a Sèvres tureen once sent me to hospital for a fortnight.' When Jeremy said that sort of thing you did not laugh, not even secretly to yourself, or afterwards with Sophie. No more than you would laugh at anyone whose contentment hung on such a narrow thread, that could so easily be snapped by the slightest accident, a fire, a burglary, sudden poverty, the kind of affliction that would distress anyone but destroy Jeremy entirely. We were all aware, I think, if that doesn't sound pretentious, of his tragic possibilities. We felt the need to protect him, to give him his heart's desires, to keep off, if we could, indefinitely, the awful chance that could ruin him.

And so we helped him get Laura, who was, I must admit, the most beautiful thing I have ever seen. So splendid that before Sophie, I had thought of her for myself – as most men would – but done nothing about it, knowing that it would take more courage than I had to ask for that perfect skin, those drowned eyes, that mermaid hair, that powerful helplessness, a look in general of something unattainable glimpsed underwater by a clumsy diver. She gave you a feeling, literally, of being out of your depth and only two things could ever give a man the courage to go after her – a madness of the deep of the most reckless type, or a need as desperate as Jeremy's for perfection.

'She sounds awful,' said Sophie when I first told her about Laura, and you couldn't blame her, hearing all that mermaid stuff about a strange woman. But that was the other thing; everyone liked Laura, even women, when they met her. She was gentle without stupidity, charming without affectation, and without apologising for it, she managed to put you at ease with her beauty so that somehow even women beside her appeared not plainer but themselves more attractive, with a borrowed or reflected loveliness that Laura succeeded in lending for a moment or two. 'Do you know,' Sophie confessed, 'I felt quite gorgeous myself, just for a second. She made my neck feel longer.' Sophie is always worried about her neck.

Not that they needed much help, for their courtship, too, was perfect. In the most delicate way Jeremy wooed her with everything he had, in his case attributes most of us have to do without, falling back instead on anything tolerable in our natures. You couldn't help but be touched by the way he won her, tempting her with his American kitchen, titillating her with his Georgian silver, astonishing her with his Impressionists, stimulating her with one sudden, stark Giacometti, finally capturing her with the French bedroom done up in blue flowered *toile de Jouy* with matching fabric on the walls, and an Empire bed. His presents too were chosen with a fine taste. Nothing vulgar nor even very expensive. Just one perfect madonna lily out of season, twelve wild strawberries in a Victorian white china plaited basket, a little grey cat with blue eyes.

They were a pleasure to watch, and they made a fine couple, as exquisitely matched as a pair of portraits painted by the same master and hung side by side. I caught a glimpse of them once, by chance, together in a restaurant, a most moving experience to anyone who is stirred by temporal beauty. We watched Jeremy pick the finest mussel from a shell on his plate and Laura extend her long throat with a swimming movement that on any other woman would have looked ridiculous, to receive it from his fork. There was something about this gesture, the way he gave and she received, that silenced the tables around them as if the diners were going to applaud. Sophie beside me blushed and I could not blame her. It was as though we had caught, unawares, two legendary beasts of great beauty, unicorns perhaps, engaged in a private rite.

'Gosh,' said Sophie, 'do you think they go on like that all the time?' and I wondered too, reflecting that marriage is both more and less than the perpetual exchange of mussels on a silver fork. He had got her all right, but what in the world was he going to do with her?

*   *   *

Why they picked on us, I don't know. Perhaps it was a supreme stroke of artistry, perhaps Jeremy felt that to make us his intimates was to add the counterpoint of ordinariness to the extraordinary quality of his own life. He and Laura were all the more vivid for our lack of colour; not that I'm running us down, don't misunderstand. By our own lights Sophie and I are bright enough. Or maybe it was simpler. We are both good-tempered. People seem to cheer up when we arrive. If you are a unicorn, with all the strain of keeping up a legend, it must be a help to have a dolphin round the house.

Whatever Jeremy's motive, after the wedding (held in a black mass chapel in Gloucestershire Jeremy especially had rededicated for the purpose), we were always in their house. It started with the delivery by messenger – Jeremy hardly ever used the telephone – of a plain white card inscribed: 'We should be so glad if you would come to see us.' No signature. But then only Jeremy could behave like that.

'What cheek,' said Sophie, but I could see she wanted to go, in fact nothing would stop her. Next to love and hatred, neither of which we felt for Jeremy, curiosity is a powerful motive. And at least, to visit them rather than the other way round, meant that apart from a tie pin and a pair of cuff links Jeremy took a fancy to, our own property was relatively safe.

And so began a strange summer.

We would have been mad, of course, not to enjoy it. The delicious food, the long Sunday mornings drinking hock and seltzer on the balcony. Sophie said, 'Hock and seltzer, does anyone drink it nowadays? I mean *does* anyone?' But she had to agree it was so much nicer than champagne. Sunday mornings were the best time of all. And best of all occasions, the moment when Laura, after breakfast in bed, made her first appearance of the day. How to describe it? What words to borrow to convey the texture of a revelation? 'Mrs Jeremy Tyndall in a drift of chiffon,' said a fashion magazine, and for once the trite, sugared words made some sort of sense. But still inadequate, limping. Certainly she wore chiffon to which she and the designer together contrived to lend the impression of a cloud. Barely surfaced from dreams or oblivion, she brought with her the faint scent of her sleep. Most people on waking smell simply unwashed. Sophie, I have always said, gives off in the early morning the not unpleasant tang of a small cosy animal that has slept in a nest of straw. Her nose is warm, her eyes damp. Laura, one felt, had lain among flowers all night and theirs was the perfume, the musky, nostalgic scent of bruised blossoms, which clung to her for a full two hours after rising.

We were hypnotised by the performance they gave. They literally played out their lives, brought to everyday existence the refining polish of art, seeming to rise above the fog in which most of us spend our days. Even in matters of the smallest importance. Before Laura's sea-green eyes, the aqueous, melting lines of that lovely face, tradesmen went mad and delivered on time, taxis sprang out of the rain, fierce dogs smiled and held their bark. In the afternoon Sophie sometimes went shopping with Laura and the account she gave of these expeditions was as good as a book.

'I couldn't believe my ears,' she said, 'they actually *offered* to deliver the same day. And I've always had to beg to be allowed to collect.

'You should have seen. When we had tea. It's like being with an angel or something. They all stopped, I mean everyone. They put down their tiny teacups and stared. And yet it wasn't rude. She simply took their breath away.

'Yet you know she's so *nice*. It's extraordinary. I always feel better after seeing Laura.'

And then later, in bed, when Sophie asked her most profound questions (the only habit she has I could do without):

'Do you think they're happy?'

I forced myself to think. Because I love Sophie and she is the only person in the world for whom I would give up my sleep. And because I felt increasingly that we had both of us, r ot exactly as friends but as witnesses, become involved in the Tyndalls' destiny. It mattered to us, as it matters to an audience at a first-class play (why did the word tragedy pass through my mind?) what became of them. Finally I made up my mind.

'Yes, my love, I think they are. I think they're happy.'

*   *   *

How was I to know I was so soon to be contradicted? As a judge of people, I have always been told, I'm pretty good. But Jeremy and Laura. They were right outside my experience, my understanding, and so when Jeremy turned up one day at our house looking like a sick dog instead of a complacent fox, I felt pity but no embarrassment at having passed a wrong judgement.

I had never expected to see him like this. Wearing his clothes badly. They were as elegant as ever (most of us have our sackcloth and ashes outfit, some unspeakable old suit and hideous tie; Jeremy simply had no such uniform in his wardrobe), but his shoes were dirty, one fly button was undone and he seemed literally to have shrunk overnight so that his collar no longer fitted.

He even failed to notice a rather nice bit of sculpture Sophie had got me for my birthday from the Feyer Gallery. 'For God's sake,' she'd said, 'don't let Jeremy see it', but she need not have bothered. Absently, he picked up a new glossy volume on the Sistine Chapel, ran his fingers over the cover, but laid it down again.

My first thought was: she's left him. He should have stuck to the inanimate. Even things are vulnerable of course. Burglary. Fire. But there is always a chance they can be saved or recovered. But people. You simply cannot collect people. Especially mermaids. With one flick of her silver tail, a flash of scales, a green look, and she's off where you cannot follow. Poor Jeremy.

'Poor Jeremy,' said Sophie, 'you look awful,' and did the practical things that women do on such occasions, getting him a drink (you would never dream of offering Jeremy a cup of tea unless the time were precisely four fifteen. It was eleven o'clock in the morning), putting a footstool under his feet, plumping up the cushion in his chair. While I thought, what on earth do you say to a man who has lost not only his wife but his most precious irreplaceable possession?

I tried to think it serves him right. One cannot go on like that. Even Jeremy. But that was the trouble. Even Jeremy could. Especially and only Jeremy, against whom, as against a man fatally crippled from birth, you cannot harden your heart. Crippled by the very fact that he lived – exquisitely – in

131

a world beautiful indeed but limited strictly to the sentient, the tangible, the visual. He had to see, to touch. Without velvet, silk, crystal, apricots for breakfast, without Laura, he was lost.

'It's Laura,' he said at last, 'she's really most frightfully ill.'

And so we were truly shocked. So shocked that it was only by getting slightly drunk beforehand that we could force ourselves to visit them. It got a bit expensive, all that gin and then a taxi to get us there because we'd left it too late for the tube. Half pickled, clutching a smoked trout or a cold bird, because Jeremy in his appalled lethargy had lost a house-keeper and failed to find another, we would turn up always hoping that things had changed for the better, that Laura and Jeremy might, overnight, have rediscovered their peculiar paradise. They were, in a way, the most innocent people I have ever known and in their garden the snake was not just a menace but an affront. Subtly, our relationship changed. Before, we had been spectators, privileged to wit-ness their life together as a fortunate ornithologist might study the mating of two rare and beautiful birds. Now it was they who studied us, searching our faces for a sign of hope, like children who cannot believe that there is no one on earth old enough and strong enough to hold at bay the annihilating darkness.

Laura's disease could not be diagnosed. She was in and out of clinics. Specialists were flown from all corners of the world, including the greatest of them all, a sardonic, simian little fellow from Switzerland who drank quantities of hock, sighed a great deal, and immediately contracted influenza. We were glad to see the back of him. The only point on which all agreed was that she was seriously, possibly fatally, ill. Her symptoms were vague and could have been those of a hun-dred ailments. She paled, she faded. Resting on her wicker chaise longue, piled with scarlet cushions, she gave the im-pression of having been cast out from her proper element, a beautiful fish-woman thrown up by the tide to die on the sand.

And while Laura sickened in the flesh, it was Jeremy who worried me most. With his languishing looks, his sighs, you would have thought it was he who was ill, and he maddened

Sophie.

'The least he could do is try to cheer her up,' she said. 'I could smack him. Take him out and get him drunk.'

That was her attitude, and understandable enough. Even praiseworthy. His behaviour, she thought, proved her suspicion, that he had never truly loved Laura. But for me it was more complicated, a matter perhaps of an imagination marginally more elastic than hers, nothing special really, but just large enough to encompass and pity a distress from which most of us, by our very ordinariness, are preserved.

I took him to Wheeler's, for if Jeremy had one devouring taste, even more highly developed than his many other vivid sensibilities, it was for shellfish, a passion he shared with Laura. When I think of them I see those two, not as traditional lovers yoked with flowers, but framed instead by an assortment of hump-backed, pearly molluscs. And no one knew as they did how to tease the pinkest, most precious morsel from the claw of the crab, the secret tenderest prize from beneath the lobster's coat of armour.

And so it was the more pathetic to see the indifference with which he tackled his scallops St Jacques, toyed with his trout.

'My dear chap,' he said, 'it really is terribly good of you. But I'm afraid I can't.' The wine he drank without even enquiring the vintage and, so far from getting drunk, he grew more sober, more melancholy with each glass.

And then, feeling perhaps that he owed me something, or more likely, because this was a confession he could no longer keep to himself:

'You know what upsets me most about this business?'

'Well.' What to say? To preserve the decencies, or speak the truth which I suspected? I settled for the first. 'The thought of losing Laura. We haven't talked about it much but I can understand . . . '

He cut me off.

'Not just losing. It's worse than that. Don't you see? Can't you see there is something worse than death?'

Obstinacy and a sudden unwillingness to hear what I knew he would confess, made me reply: 'Offhand I can't think of anything.'

He pushed aside his strawberries, finished his wine with

the grimace of a man swallowing down brackish water:

'The flaw. Surely you can see that. The fatal flaw. I thought she was perfect.'

Jeremy Tyndall, a man for whom to show even the faintest surprise in public was a flagrant exhibitionism, laid his face in his hands, and wept.

A month later I was sent to Italy to set up an export office in Milan. Sophie came with me and it was with a mixture of anxiety and relief that we left behind the Tyndalls and their problems. Secretly I think neither of us expected to see Laura alive again. We hardly mentioned them, partly because under the Italian sun death and heartbreak in Chelsea seemed mercifully far away, obscured by a hundred new experiences, including Sophie's pregnancy; partly because this was one of the few topics that made us quarrel. We who had never indulged in the sex war ('I mean it's so silly,' Sophie used to say, 'people are just people'), found ourselves assuming postures we would once have thought ridiculous. There was a time when our attitude to the Tyndalls had been one, a bond. Now any mention of them led always to the same conclusion, a state of war in which Sophie, bristling with indignation, swept Laura's lovely shadow off to her end of the field, while unhappily, but irresistibly, I took Jeremy's part. So much, I thought, for detachment. Grief is a sticky thing.

'I found a lovely bit of glass,' Sophie said, 'I thought I'd send it to Laura.' She groaned and put up her feet. 'Get me a drink, there's a love.

'Well don't you want to see it? I carted my tum round all afternoon to find it.' Absently she patted her pregnancy, which we called Fred.

'I wish you wouldn't. The heat. And Fred.' But Fred was not to save us. No jokes.

'I may be pregnant but I'm not dying. You might at least look.' On guard.

'It's beautiful. They'll adore it.'

'They? It's for her, not him.' She knocked down her Campari in one and glowered. There is nothing more formidable than a pregnant woman on her back with a drink inside her and a quarrel to pick.

With the air of someone with all the time in the world to tear you limb from limb, she waved her glass for more.

'How can you be so heartless?'

'It's not that I don't care about her.' Fool.

'Anyone would think.'

'But I'm sorry for him. I don't think you quite understand.'

'There's nothing to understand. He disgusts me.' Small arms. Cannons coming up.

'Don't you mind at all about her? Do you mind about anything? If she died? If I died?' Confuse the enemy with smokescreen.

'That has nothing to do with it.' One minute amnesty. Sulks and silence. I spilled the ice on the floor.

'Now look what you've done.'

'If you want to know I do care. I wanted to marry her once.' The unspeakable spoken. Tears. I'm a beast. Comfort. Apologies (mine, of course). More tears. Another drink. Fred-talk. Peace. For a while.

A year later we came home bringing with us Fred, who turned out to be Freda and actually Caroline, a smattering of Italian, some pretty bits and pieces, a taste for *saltimbocca romana*, and the sober but not too fearful realisation that within the walls of our invulnerable marriage there was at least one small area of darkness in which we could totally misunderstand each other. But there are bear traps in every marriage and neither of us was so complacent as to imagine that we could escape them forever. Or so feeble as to fear that the Tyndalls could break us up.

Getting back put things in perspective. Now, setting aside our quarrel, we were joined again by one feeling: a simple reluctance to see them again.

'At least she's not dead,' said Sophie, 'or we'd have heard.'

What we didn't say was how much we dreaded becoming once more involved in their lives, or rather their death, for getting ready to visit them for the first time felt more like preparing for a funeral. Sophie, I noticed, put on a red dress and too much make-up. I got a bit drunk.

What we found will give me food for thought for the rest

of my life, convinced me of the limitations of my own imagination, my arrogance in assuming that I could grasp and contain in my mind the size and shape of any human feeling outside my experience. The lengths to which an obsession can go, blotting out all other sensations, bringing pain to which the more happily adjusted are strangers, and comfort in a situation which would be the end of most of us. The motives, the roots of such an obsession are beyond me. In a sense I envy it. To have one such powerful driving force to every thought and action. It's like destiny.

In Laura there was little change. She had slipped further into the shadows. She was as beautiful as ever. We were prepared for this. What astonished us was Jeremy: like a dusty bird after a shower of rain he had regained his glossy plumage. Once again his belly filled his trousers, his waistcoat was more exotic than ever. He had prepared for us a steaming dish of *moules marinières*. He was not just himself again. He was more than himself. He had had the house entirely redecorated in *trompe l'oeil* – 'Old hat, dear boy, but I fancied it.' What had been blank walls were now vistas of Versailles. I smashed my nose on the lavatory door, a perfect photographic representation of the hall of mirrors. Most remarkable was the bedroom where Laura lay, done up like the principal bedchamber in the Petit Trianon. One whole wall of the drawing room was a view of formal gardens and artificial pools.

'I'm glad,' I said, when we were alone after dinner in what had been his study, was now an olive grove, 'to see you so well.'

'Never been better,' he said.

'But Laura,' I said, and need not have asked. He would have told me anyway. 'Have they diagnosed her illness? Do they know what's the matter?'

'My dear fellow, yes. That's the whole point.'

'She'll get better then?'

'Well yes. Perhaps no. They don't know.' He got up from his desk, moved a paperweight (Fabergé, I think) precisely one quarter of an inch, and explained.

'We had this chap from Russia. The only one in the world who knows, a really splendid fellow. Such a fuss, of course, with the Foreign Office, but worth every penny. She has a disease of the blood, probably incurable. In the whole world it's the only known case. Unique. Perfect.

'You might call it a collector's piece.'

I took Sophie home in a hurry and made love to her. It was all very pleasant and familiar. As passion goes, I prefer the everyday.

1968

17

The Saint of Islington Green

'Retired you say?'

'More like stopped. Stopped, that's what I'd say. Just shut up the shop, came round the back and put on his slippers just as usual and said, Right, Rosie, I've done. That's my lot. At his age, with his responsibilities.'

Rosie opened up her great flower face – her name was right, her mother might have known that in her prime she would look like this, a big-faced hybrid tea towards the end of the season – she opened her face for sympathy, comfort, a word to heal her incurable sorrows. The landlord pushed another port across the bar, it was understood to be on the house. Rosie today was like April, she had been crying and she would cry again; the port brought a thin sun to her face but there would soon be another shower.

I was rather pleased with the hybrid tea. I scribbled it on my cuff – I wear paper cuffs in readiness for such rare moments when a word or a phrase that has been itching suddenly and beautifully reveals itself. It would not have done to carry a notebook; people, I have observed, lose spontaneity when they see you writing things down. But it was very important that I should miss nothing, for Islington was really my last resort: as a writer I enjoy a certain facility with words and a boundless curiosity, but I lack invention and memory. I had come to live in Islington – that was before it got smart – in the hope that if I kept very still and opened my ears and eyes I should collect almost without effort something of value. Of course you scavenge a lot of rubbish along with the jewels and you have to wait a long time for something to happen, but that afternoon in the pub the sense of something happening at last was so strong I itched right down to the soles of my feet. The price of observation is that you cannot afford to scratch, you must hold yourself back and keep your passion to yourself. I wore, most of the time, a face of kindly interest and people quite often told me things. I never gave advice but I had learned to show the manners of a listener. When Rosie left, I followed her.

It was really very interesting how Harry Rosetti became a saint.

One night he just shut up shop, as usual, and said Right, Rosie, I've done, that's my lot. At first – Rosie told me as I walked beside her, me with one shoulder slightly bent towards her in a sort of stooping benevolence, encouraging, I hoped – at first she had not understood. It had not seemed the sort of remark expecting an answer yes or no, nor a statement that was going to turn anybody's life – hers and the children's – inside out and upside down. That seemed to annoy her most of all, that she had let Harry's remark, a catastrophe, slip by under her nose. It had been some time before she realised what Harry meant, that he wasn't going to work any more, that he had stopped.

He sat there in his prime – he, like Rosie, was at his best in these, the middle years of his life – wearing his slippers. We all went to see him, filing in turn into the little back room which was also the kitchen, to find out for ourselves. He was a fine-looking fellow with the strength in his arms of his country-bred Italian parentage and the curly black hair of the South. You would never have suspected him of harbouring an aberration if you had seen him before, behind his counter, flashing his gold teeth for the ladies and fondling with his great hands, on which the black hair curled, the still warm pizzas from Rosie's oven, a speciality of the shop. Or if you did credit him with having something remarkable up his sleeve, you would have guessed at some more active eccentricity – a love affair or some exuberant murder performed without malice out of sheer delight in his strength.

To his visitors he was impeccably polite but indifferent, and to his children, who accepted more readily than their mother the change in circumstances, he was kind but absent-minded. While they climbed all over their mountainous father, he treated them like puppies, he the sleeping dog, brushing off one with a great paw, embracing another. Rosie, meanwhile, was angry. While Harry received his visitors like a king, she seethed over her cooking, serving spaghetti without oil, a desperate gesture which failed still to awaken the new, mysterious Harry. His appetite was as big as ever, but he seemed not to notice what he was eating. 'And well,' said Rosie, 'I can't starve him, can I?' as if she wanted to.

Rosie never spoke when Harry had visitors but she followed us out through the shop and more than made up for her silence with a torrent of words which held not so much reproach as utter bewilderment at this reversal in her life. She would number her six children, by ages downwards from twelve to two, shedding always a special tear for the last, the youngest, abandoned so inexplicably by its father. 'Not me,' she would say, 'not for me but the baby,' and I believed her. To witness Rosie's distress was like being caught in a thunderstorm. Her grief, which fed and watered itself, had swollen within her from a shower to a gale and you could have drowned in it.

'Rosie,' I said to Harry one evening, feeling it was my duty, 'is very unhappy. You have upset her.' I had become almost his only visitor. After their first curiosity, the others had fallen off, either from fear of Rosie's grief or from disappointment. They had expected to find Harry ill or mad, but he was neither. Only I persevered, for that was my job. 'Already,' I added, 'she is obliged to take food from the shop. You cannot expect it of her.'

There had been a time, before he stopped, when Harry would rise like a great grinning fish to the most insubstantial remark. Out of joy he would pursue with delight the slightest proposition from a word about the weather to an examination of the nature of the universe. Now he simply smiled with a massive patience which Rosie must have found very irritating.

'I am thinking,' he said, 'of going to bed.'

'But you're not ill are you? Why on earth do you want to go to bed?'

'There is a proper way,' he said, rather primly, 'of doing these things.' That was what he used to say about the pizzas, when people asked him for the secret.

'But what are you doing, Harry?'

'You will see,' he said, 'in time you will understand, all of you.'

I lost touch with the Rosetti affair for a while because something else came up. I was actually given a commission to do a job for a newspaper. I think they had got me mixed up with somebody. But for a time I only heard, in the pub, how Harry and Rosie were getting on. Rosie had got her mother-in-law from looking after a priest in Clerkenwell to help her run the shop. Harry had gone to bed and become an outcast in his own family. Neither his mother nor his wife would talk to him and the children were kept from his room. They fed him and that was all. I can't say I blamed them, nor did anyone, for after their first hesitation, everyone in the Green had come down firmly on Rosie's side. She could always be sure of a sympathetic port whenever she went to the pub, and now she had managed to subdue the torrent of her indignation, and wore instead a face of patient endurance, she had become a figure of universal pity. Almost a heroine. Until Father Fox turned up.

There was, it turned out later, no mystery at all about Father Fox's appearance in the pub. If he seemed to materialise rather than opening the door and coming in like everybody else, that was simply the way he had of entering a room, pausing for a second outside and then running the last bit with a sort of sideways crab-like gait. If the more impressionable reported an aura about him, it may have been the scent of the church that clung to him. I had a personal theory, that he put incense behind his ears. Any mystery that was left was exploded when I discovered that his cousin was the very same priest that Rosie's mother-in-law had looked after in Clerkenwell. But there were those, particularly of the Virgin's faith, who clung for many years to the conviction that there was something miraculous about Father Fox. They told their children, who will probably tell their own children and their grandchildren. I have even heard about Father Fox in

Northampton, told to me as though I hadn't been on the spot
when he appeared, by a woman who sold twenty Players to a
long-distance bus driver from Victoria who knew Rosie's
uncle.

Still you didn't have to be feeble-minded to be impressed
by his first entrance into the Islington Dog. He was preceded
by a cold wind (it was chilly for July) which blew him like a
leaf and left him faintly quivering in the middle of the public
bar. He always had a look of frailty, as if he was halfway to
Heaven and liable to take off at any moment on the last
flight. People used to carry small parcels for him and ask him
to Sunday dinner, and I have even seen a woman in her
eighth month give up a seat to him on a bus. He took it
beautifully. Only I knew and had not the heart to tell, that in
the Midlands where he came from he had sent to their Holy
Father (from self-defence) a sixteen-stone weight-lifter who
had tried to pinch the sacramental wine. In view of the
Father's obvious frailty and the other man's strength, a
Roman Catholic magistrate had packed the priest off home
with a substantial cheque for his church.

We had been warming up for a sing-song, but we all
stopped to watch and to listen as, taking his time, he paused,
then skipped across to George at the bar. With a Guinness in
his hand, he paused again, then pecked at the froth like a
bird at a water bowl. We had to lean forward to catch what he
said (that was a trick he had, to make you reach to catch his
whisper, as if he had lost his voice; it gave weight to the
lightest remark):

'Has anyone,' he said, 'seen Harry Rosetti?'

Rosie in the corner drew in her breath and blushed like a
bride, seemed about to speak then held her tongue. Then
suddenly, released from their enraptured silence, everyone
was talking, telling him, rushing to explain. Only I stayed
behind and only I saw Rosie, her lips tight, and her flower
face closed up, slip from the bar behind their backs, just as if
she knew what was going to happen.

Rosie, of course, was bound to lose. She had never been a
quick mover, she had too much weight to carry, and things
happened so fast that all she could do was pant along behind
and hope that somehow, as miraculously as her ordeal had

begun, it would end. But what could she do against God and Father Fox? For Harry Rosetti had become a saint.

'Not canonised exactly, you understand,' Father Fox whispered to me in the pub one evening of such blinding autumn beauty that you could almost believe in saints, even I, with the bar turned to gold and the clatter of leaves against the window, 'not yet canonised. But a saint as clearly as our little flower of Avila. It is given.' It must have been the light but I had to admit that there was something golden, that night, about Father Fox: 'It is given to few to see in their own lifetime, a saint. They are simple people.' His pale gaze seemed to embrace not only the drinkers around us but the entire population of the Green and beyond, almost the whole earth: 'but I think – I believe – ' he seemed to imply that his pride was a poor thing but sanctified, 'that I have brought them to understand.' You always felt, somehow, with Father Fox, that he had a special relationship with God. I would not have been surprised if he rang him up on the telephone.

They had understood. They went to see Harry again, not in their dozens, but their twenties and their hundreds from as far as Chelsea, to lay at his bedside little bunches of flowers, bowls of soup, breast of chicken, angel cake, and the children their favourite toys. And they never failed to drop a coin in the palm of Father Fox who had opened their eyes to a miracle. For them, Harry was Heaven, and Father Fox St Peter at the gate. While Harry's great muscles shrank and dissolved and his skin took on the texture of paper, Father Fox was interviewed by the newspapers and had a letter from Rome. They were after Rosie too, it was somehow expected that she would become a nun, but she ran from them and hid, and her flesh too fell from her like petals from a flower. She hid in my room and I wished, for once, that I was the sort of person who gave advice. I made us instant coffee and we kept ourselves apart, each for different reasons, from the terrible magic of Father Fox and Rosie's sainted husband.

Autumn burned itself out and the gold, spent, gave way to a snapping snarling winter of wind and rain. A high official came in a Bentley from the Vatican after a sea crossing, and Father Fox dissolved, as mysteriously as he had come, in a convenient fog. They took Harry to hospital and gave the children back their toys, as many as they could trace. Rosie went off, not to a nunnery, but to the warm arms of a commercial traveller in spaghetti. People still talk about Father Fox, especially in July, but they hardly remember Harry. I think about him sometimes, but that's my job.

1962

18

Reflections

'The new waiter?'

'Yes?'

'I have the impression he wears a wig. And yet it is white.'

'That is nothing to me,' says the proprietor. 'He is efficient. He is working his way up.'

'Also, he rubs his upper lip as though he were missing a moustache.'

The restaurant on the Avenida is, as it has ever been, the sober-sided refuge of the middle classes who prefer things to be as they have ever been, and there is nothing wrong with that. All around there is change and mostly decay – what with the junkies and the muggers and the takeaway Chinese – but the moment you close the door of the restaurant behind you and walk through the bead curtain, what solace there is in the brown and muted decency. New paper tablecloths every morning, on each table the Martini ashtray, a single carnation that wilts through the week from Saturday to Friday and the carafe of water, though most clients prefer mineral water or the light fizzy beer of the country. (There is little demand for wine: the local white is over-sweet and the red rusty to the teeth – the copper, or some other mineral in the soil, one says, enters the vine from the root; the French does not travel well or, having travelled, sickens; besides, one would wake from one's siesta with vinous gravel in the mouth or rage in the head. There is work to be done. Now, more than ever, work must be seen to be done.)

There has always been the electric fan, the walls have always been brown, the mirrors reflect everything that goes on in the restaurant on the Avenida. A famous poet came here once, and he was reflected, also his harlot. No dogs are allowed and therefore they are not reflected, though there is the old actress who brings her cat and feeds it raw *bifteck* on a fondue fork. She was once a belle and in those days when she came in for an after-theatre supper the mirrors reflected her beauty, but they do not remember it. Mirrors are unforgiving.

There is a writer, also, everyone respects and no one reads (myself), but he dresses like a doctor or a solicitor (to confuse the mirrors?). A painter comes here too, a lemony fellow who draws murderously on the paper tablecloths. But neither the actress nor the writer nor the painter is representative of the clientele, who are solid accountants and store-owners or managers and dentists and actuaries and civil servants. Their reflections are irreproachable. In the middle of the day they wag their heads over the newspapers. In the evening many call in for a beer or a *fine* at the stainless steel bar with the Cappuccino machine and on Fridays they buy a lottery ticket. Sometimes they bring their wives and families here for dinner (hardly ever their mistresses, because of the reflections).

There is a recess across which curtains may be drawn for private parties but mostly it is the staff who eat here, about three o'clock and also at midnight.

Gruber's feet do not seem too good but, as the proprietor says, he will rise. At first he never had much to say but he is the hardest worker I have ever seen. By seven in the morning he is sweeping out the restaurant and he is still there at midnight. Where he sleeps is a wonder. He might be the loneliest man I have ever seen.

Gruber looks a little like Chaplin in his last years, but more vigorous. He wears a white jacket, black trousers, a little black tie, and he takes particular pleasure in polishing the mirrors: he works away with leather and vinegar water like a window cleaner – you might almost believe there was a view beyond to be revealed.

Thus, one day at three forty the restaurant on the Avenida is empty, but for Gruber, who wrings out his leather and vinegar for the last time and brings me a *fine* on a tray, in a glass, on a paper mat on a saucer.

'You work very hard, Gruber. Yourself?'

'Thank you, sir. A beer.'

'If you will join me. You are rising, Gruber.'

'I believe so, sir. My step-brother was in the same trade, but he did not rise. You can imagine my age, sir? I am eighty-nine.'

'Eighty-nine is a great age for anyone and for a waiter working his way up it is miraculous. For most people. For the majority.'

'The majority represents not only ignorance but cowardice. The majority can never replace the man.'

'Indeed.'

Rubbing his upper lip in the familiar gesture, Gruber appears to weigh me (for the first time I notice his extraordinarily piercing eyes – normally lowered as he goes about his duties). Satisfied, he speaks confidentially. His voice is a little harsh. He has an air of authority and I guess this is not the first time in his life he has been on the rise. I wonder if he has been a schoolmaster or even a captain of industry. One does not ask Gruber such questions. As he talks he rearranges the table to his satisfaction: the salt cellar is apparently a little out of line, the water carafe must be centred, exactly so.

'This place, for instance, is anarchic. I intend to initiate some reforms. You are startled, sir, I can see that. But my propositions will be acceptable to the proprietor. I have persuaded him that the kitchen staff – not to mention those who wait upon table – will welcome a firm hand. The psyche of the broad masses is accessible only to what is strong and uncompromising. That has been my experience.'

'You have considerable experience of catering, Mr Gruber?'

'Not of catering, sir; but of human nature, yes.'

After this first interview Gruber and I have many such chats (this appears to be his only weakness – the need for a confidant). In fact, it is he who tends to initiate the conversations and – I realise – set the subject. I am amazed by the old waiter's grasp of politics, history, music, art, architecture.

The proprietor falls ill and gives Gruber leave to carry through his programme of reforms. The service improves, the food no longer arrives tepid at the table. Gruber no longer sweeps out in the morning or washes the mirrors – he has underlings to do this now. There is a spring in his step, he looks younger, he snaps his fingers for service and begins to spend more time with the customers. With the staff he becomes positively tyrannical, and, overhearing his way with a sloppy cook, a waiter whose paper cuffs are not fresh that morning, the fish chef who has been caught spitting in the *bouillabaisse* and sacked without notice, I ask Gruber how it is that he appears to inspire and retain unusual loyalty? What I mean is – and I think he understands – the serving classes will not put up nowadays with autocracy.

'Then,' he says, with a smile almost sly, 'they may go elsewhere for a job.'

'But there are no jobs to be had.'

'Exactly.'

Another time.

'You're a monster, Gruber. You're working them to death.'

'The masses are scarcely conscious of the fact that their freedom as human beings is abused. They feel very little shame at being terrorised intellectually. You would agree these are bad times?'

(Who could deny that?)

'I have history on my side. They will do as they are told. And my customers? Have you heard any complaints that the omelettes are light and the plates are hot?'

The proprietor dies. Gruber takes over the restaurant. He puts on weight and it turns out that he is not, after all, alone in the world. At half past three or at midnight, he dines with a crony in the staff recess. We do not have so many talks nowadays. It is autumn, then it is winter. The leaves fall from the trees in the Avenida, awnings are taken in, and pavement tables; a cold wolf of a wind blows from the *sierra*, the old actress dies and will never more be reflected. Her little cat is found in the alley behind the restaurant, its neck broken. I do not sleep so well and at midnight wrap up, push my flask into

148

my pocket and pace the Retiro Park and the Avenida. I think of flying out, but there are hijackings almost every day and a strike at the airport, broken up by the militia – but there is now no one to fly the planes. And then the militia strike. There are riots: pointless when there is no militia to put them down. This is a bad season for everyone but Gruber, who flourishes. He buys up the restaurant across the Avenida, then a couple more in the city. I hear that these deals are not altogether straight, that Gruber has brought pressure to bear, that he has connections with some organisation that is not entirely legal (though who is to say, nowadays, what is and is not legal?). Gruber puts up his prices. Some of the old customers disappear. One day they are there, the next they are not. The painter, I notice, has been moved from his corner table to one by the serving door and he no longer draws on the tablecloths. I still retain my place (by grace perhaps of the many interesting chats I have had with Gruber on all kinds of subjects) and so can still see, when the curtain is not drawn, the recess where the staff used to eat about three o'clock and midnight, reflected in a mirror on the opposite wall. But the staff no longer eat there – instead Gruber holds court for an increasing number of intimates (I had no idea he had so many friends in this city). For these cronies nothing apparently is too good: fantastical ice creams, the whole roast head of a pig, lobster out of season, wines imported by air, black-market Cuban cigars, oysters, ortolan. Well, Gruber deserves it – he has risen.

He still spares a little time for me, for the sake of the good talks we have had. In spite of the company he keeps, the servant turned master still strikes me as a lonely soul.

'I am a self-educated man,' he says. 'This is not the first time I have risen. But I must tell you, my friend, at my age it becomes tiring to work one's way up.'

'You're healthier than I am, Gruber.'

'Ah, that cough. Might I prescribe rum and lemon? With a little honey?'

Gruber is right about the cough. For a few weeks I am away from the restaurant then resume my insomniac night walks, though I am probably not fit to go out. A slight fever keeps me warm, I sit in the park, then around the middle of the night find myself shivering in the Avenida. I take my accustomed table in the empty restaurant and, waiting for the barman to bring me a *café filtre* and a cognac, I look up and see reflected in the mirror, dining in the recess, a jolly party: Adolf Hitler, Goebbels, Bormann, Goering, Himmler, the six Goebbels children – Hela, Hilda, Helmut, Holde, Hedda and Heide (who should be in bed by now) – and Adolf's dog the great Alsatian, Blondi – the first dog ever to be reflected in the restaurant on the Avenida. It's bitter out, there is snow in the wind. Nearly Christmas. The conifers on the *sierra* will have had their first frosting and the air will be very clear and bright. I gulp my cognac and run home.

Of course, it is absurd: some waking dream or hallucination. Still, I keep away from the restaurant in the Avenida, nurse my cough and take my exercise in the Retiro Park. Even in winter it is a pleasant place: a few nurses still bring their charges here to play, there are the pink-stockinged flamingoes on the lake and cheerful ducks. I carry bread for the ducks and nuts for the squirrels.

One afternoon just before Christmas I find the gaunt painter from the restaurant in the Avenida sketching the Retiro flamingoes. He's a dry fellow with whom, in all the years at the restaurant, I have never exchanged more than a nod, but on an impulse I take a place next to him on the bench. We sit in silence for a while.

'Tell me, how are our friends in the Avenida?'

'I no longer go there. It is not a happy place – except, of course, for Gruber and his pals.'

He explains: from his table by the serving door he overheard the so-correct Gruber shouting at the kitchen staff. Prices went up, the quality of the food went down. As for himself – it was made clear that he was no longer welcome. First the table by the serving door, then a dirty tablecloth, a cockroach in his soup. Finally he was told that no table was available, even by the serving door.

The next day we meet again. We take a *café-cognac* at the small bar in the Retiro Park, standing at the counter. My new friend, etiolated, could be a flamingo himself, roosting on one leg. He wears mittens to sketch outdoors in winter. He tells me there are rumours that Gruber is running a protection racket. He also tells me that for many years when they were younger, he was the lover of the actress with the cat – though she had no cat then (extraordinary, these unlooked-for connections one discovers by chance, like secret passages in a house).

He talks of painting, I of books.

'I wonder, did you ever read a story by Isaac Bashevis Singer – or someone – about seeing Hitler and his buddies dining in a New York restaurant?'

'No, I never read that story.'

A few days later, sitting on our bench on a raw, grey afternoon, I think again of the conifers on the *sierra*, of decorated trees and childhood.

'What will you be doing for Christmas?'

My friend snaps his sketchbook shut. His coat, I think, though once good, is too thin for this weather.

'I do not regard Christmas. I am a Jew.'

Previously alien in this Catholic, southern hemisphere, Santa has somehow got a work permit and drives his sleigh down the Avenida chuckling 'ho ho ho'. Some desperation has seized the city and in these bad times he has more customers than the Virgin or her sweetly scented crèche in the porch of the cathedral. The shops are brilliant, everyone throws their money away like dirt, which it nearly is. This is old Claus's Christmas and he rides through the town like Bacchus, frightening children. There are drunks around Christmas Eve; with the crowds still in the streets at eleven and the electronic Christmas peal of bells from Flores, the big store on the Avenida, there is an air of terrible carnival. There is a firemen's strike and at midnight the restaurant on the Avenida is burned to the ground. Someone with a grudge. Maybe that fish chef who was sacked for spitting in the *bouillabaisse*. It must have been someone with inside knowledge, to pick a time when only Gruber would be there, with his friends. No one survives. The militia break in with axes and shatter all the mirrors, every one.

*   *   *

Spring in the Retiro, a light like gauze, soft air, children with balloons and pets, nurses in tow. The local currency, too, is buoyant again and at the Retiro bar old belles gossip over their cream pastries; there is a new restaurant in the Avenida but I prefer to share my lunch with the ducks and drowse and hear the nurses call.

A big dog nearly topples me and is called off by one of the children. I don't mind. I like dogs.

'What's his name?'

'Blondi.'

And I hear the nurses call after the children: 'Hela, come here! Hilda, Helmut, Holde! Hedda! Heide!'

1980

19

Going Home

He woke to find her shaking his arm. He felt that his chest
was crushed beneath a hoop of iron. He lay still waiting for it
to shift.

'You were shouting. Was it the dream again?' Her face was
a pale disc above him. He pushed himself up then swung his
legs out from under the sheets so that he was sitting on the
edge of the bed, his back to her. Breathing was better now,
the sweat dried coldly on him. She sank back but did not close
her eyes. 'You should see someone. It's not just the dreams.
Aren't you getting in again?'

'Not worth it.' He walked round the end of the bed to the
door and put out his hand but he only touched her shoulder.
'Go back to sleep.'

In the small room where Sally had slept when she was a
baby – they had not been in this house when Michael was
born – he put on the same suit he had worn to work yesterday. After he had gone to bed his wife had hung it up and
put out a clean shirt and a clean pair of socks. Opening the
louvred cupboard doors to find a tie, he snuffed a closeted,
powdery sharpness, hers.

There was a remarkable clarity, everything more than
usually defined. He flicked a switch on the control-board by
the oven and a light came on at the base of the coffee
percolator. The refrigerator hummed into its cycle. The table
was laid for breakfast. When the cornflakes were finished,
but not before, Michael would be allowed to cut out the
month's offer and send 30p for the Mr Spock ray-gun. Sally

still used her baby bowl. He read: 'Bobby Bear went to the Moon one day, Fishing for Starfish I've heard say.' No message there. Pot of hyacinths on the dresser, too pink, blindingly sweet. School term dates, notice about PTA meeting pinned up on red felt-covered board with Mick's latest masterpiece: two massive tanks on collision course, jet fighters, big-bellied bombers laying bombs like eggs, very small stick-insect people, black. Papers on mat: bombs, Ireland, floods, famine, drought, Rod Stewart marriage on/off/on.

The garden was full of sun, tarpaulin still over the sand-pit but bulbs pushing through already. The corner of the lawn was in shadow. He saw himself cross the bright grass and sit on a deckchair in the shed. His wife did not go there. Spades clotted with earth, paperback Orwell surviving its second winter here and the attentions of mice. *I should not like to be shot for having an intelligent face, but I do agree that in almost any revolt the leaders would tend to be people who could pronounce their aitches.* Can't drop my aitches now, used to, sometimes if I'm drunk, my party turn. The shed smelled of his father, who had never seen it. There was a bit of wood Michael had been trying out his new penknife on, shaping something. He picked it up, tried to follow the wavering intentions of his son's imagination, and put it in his pocket. His heart broke.

She would think he'd gone off early.

He saw her with the children in the kitchen, lit from here like a stage. She was softer in the morning, blurred, she wandered around the kitchen in her housecoat giving the children breakfast, drinking coffee, lit a cigarette, squinted into the sun: Michael went alone to the primary round the corner, Sally would be picked up and carried off to nursery school.

The children left. She sat down, lit another cigarette, poured more coffee, then she got up and scraped the plates into the bin, picked up the papers, sat down. A small neat woman, dark, who could never quite make up her mind if her womb hampered or fulfilled her — her only bewilderment, a touching one. She looked at the *Guardian*, frowned, wondering what was the matter with her husband.

*   *   *

154

He slipped out through the little gate at the end of the garden and got into his car. Driving through the suburbs, he was dazzled as he had been on waking by the crashing brilliance of minutiae: a child's anorak throbbed red, a man standing on a pedestrian overpass, like a country stroller watching a river, was haloed in light. At a traffic block in Mill Hill a long black Mercedes drew up alongside him. He saw a child with eyes like toffee, two veiled women wearing white gloves, and a wolfhound. At the same moment they all turned and looked at him.

At any time he might have changed his mind and taken his bursting heart back to the woman in the kitchen. *I cannot breathe in this electric house in this city, this marriage, though I love you most dearly: the years lie on my breast like sand.* He could have said. Since time had struck him dumb he had conducted many such unspeakable monologues in his mind addressed to wife, children, father, friends, strangers, the living and the dead. Now the M1 peeled away before him, a straight line north, home. Home? He settled back in his seat, flicked the radio to Vivaldi and felt the iron hoops ease. He breathed better, was aware of hunger.

He saw himself. His spirit cruised comfortably above him like an angel, observed how cleverly he parked the car, pushed open the glass doors, walked to the counter, took a tray and, accompanied by his angel, set out on the table eggs, bacon, sausages, tomatoes, tea, thick white bread and butter. Children's high-tea food. Nancy and I do not eat breakfast in the electric house. Up cholesterol. The artery walls thicken leading to sluggish circulation and heart failure. Ah, the heart is a tender, treacherous organ, a brave little pump bearing one up mountains, through a number of energetic beds (the act of love equivalent to a five-mile walk), but so terribly subject to breaking. And aching. My father's burst as he walked down the summer garden path to cut a cabbage. He was a small, neat, faithful man, with dry hands.

Some old men die in bed with young mistresses. Infidelity strains the heart.

So does time, obesity, smoking, anger and responsibility.

'Aren't you going to eat that?'

She looked like all the young do nowadays: hair that might have been gold tormented into a wild frizz, half Afro, half Burne-Jones; a paisley smock thing, the kind of garment worn long ago by good children bowling hoops in picture books; duffle bag; grubby purple crochet shawl; twang of Cockney in her accent – classless, the way they all talk now. Good strong face though, clear gaze.

'Because if you aren't, could I have it?'

Preposterous. Bloody cheek. But then, why not? He pushed the plate towards her, went on smoking. She ate fast but thoroughly, with the fastidious energy of a cat. No thanks, but equally, no offence. A clean transaction, no strings. He took pains not to be watching her (why?), lit another cigarette, looked at the electric clock over the Formica bar. A man who gives away breakfasts must have somewhere to go.

'Will you give me a lift?'

'You don't know where I'm going.'

'Doesn't matter.'

He shrugged.

'Which is your car?'

'That one.'

'Nice.'

She walked out ahead of him to the car. Her feet were bare, but quite clean. She settled in the seat, experimented, lowered it till she was nearly lying flat, stretched her legs out straight, closed her eyes. His angel, who had condoned his flight, so helpfully escorted him thus far to a sensible breakfast, pardoned even his anorexia, saw this latest rashness as a motorway pick-up, unworthy of the high adventure. Sourly, he folded his wings.

She awoke without shock, as the young can, as he imagined she always did. She had a very faint golden down, he noticed, all over her skin.

'Why do you smoke so much?' There was a freshness about her, she asked questions because she genuinely wanted answers, just as she had wanted the breakfast. *Free* came into his mind, and *brave*.

'Habit, I suppose. Filthy habit.' Programmed, defensive responses. We've all got to go. At least I don't rape little girls

or beat my wife. Nan so forbearing. No one smoked nowadays. Darling, find Daddy's ciggies.

'Do you like it?'

'I hate it.'

'Then throw it away.'

'No.' Bugger you, child, with your open face.

She liked that. Surprise. For the first time she smiled. She
flicked on the radio with her toe and Beethoven came belting
out. *Tarara-boom-di-ay . . . I'm sitting on a tomb-di-ay.* Sweet, sad
Chekhov, fifteen years ago with Nan at the Lyric, Ham-
mersmith. He found that he was laughing. The bright
road peeled away. They set behind them wedges of England,
began to enter his country.

'Bradbury. Alan Bradbury.'

'Mandy.'

'Amanda?'

'Miranda.'

They ate pies as they went along. He did not want to go
into houses. She had a bottle of water in her duffle bag.

'Good. You've cheered up. You had a long face back there.'
She asked questions but made no demands. He could have
stopped the car, reached across to open the door and told her
to get out. He had a comfortable feeling of himself in the car,
a riding soul in a chariot on a road on the planet in space. He
wanted to tell her this.

Bradbury named the town to which they were going. 'I'm
an architect. There might be a site.'

A slight impatient nod. She knew this was not the whole
story. As they put the miles behind them he felt Nan and the
children grow smaller until they seemed to be waving from a
little raft.

The motorway ran through a deep cutting. He turned off
into a feed-road which started broad then narrowed and
climbed, setting them on an eminence above a valley. The
trees were still black here and sparse, there was a snap of
snow in the air. Bradbury was a heavy man: his thick corded
neck acknowledged the weight of his head; in the south he
lumbered, displacing too much territory; here, in the open,
on the hard ground, his gravity was right.

The girl sat to the left of him and a little behind on a dry-stone wall, with the car rug draped round her shoulders. Her face was pinched with cold, almost ugly, the strong planes sharpened. He turned back and smiled, choosing to be anxious for her.

'You'll get frozen.'

She slipped off the wall and came up behind him. She rested one hand lightly on his shoulder, with the other held the rug around her. Across the valley a black town was piled on the hill. There was no colour at all in the landscape but Bradbury was eased as if he were sitting before his own hearth.

The girl said: 'I've never been this far before.'

He couldn't believe it.

'Oh, all over, of course, North Africa, Spain. I lived in Spain – that was all right.' She explained: 'But I've never been up here. It's different, isn't it? You look different when you're looking at it. You come from here, don't you?'

He nodded.

Back in the car, Bradbury felt a sudden spit of temper towards the girl, because she had seen how he felt. He wanted to be angry with her.

'Why don't you wear shoes? You ought to wear shoes.'

'Why?'

'Because your feet will get cold.'

She smiled, fiddled with the radio and began to hum. They drove on. She curled up on the bench seat, her offending feet tucked under her. She turned up the radio. Something raw and rackety. Bradbury snapped it off, drove stiff-faced.

The girl was laughing at him.

'You shouldn't do this,' he said. 'Hitch lifts from men.'

'Are you going to rape me?' Not coy or even remotely provocative, just straight out, wanting to know. 'I wouldn't mind if you did.'

'Then it wouldn't be rape, would it?'

'I could put up a fight?'

'Not today, thanks.'

'What's she like?'

'Who?'

'Your wife.'

At this point the mill-stream ran by the road, on the other side the river: fast cold water over stone. His father walked by the river on a summer evening – look, boy, a dragonfly. At this point, as you entered the valley, it was like going through a passage, between walls of granite. Bradbury pulled in just before the bridge. He felt nothing.

He leaned across and opened the car door. 'Get out,' he said.

It was dark when he got into town. The one good inn had changed – all flash and Formica – but they could put him up. Why should it not have changed? Why should they know him? He had thought of the past contained, in pockets of time.

In his room he flopped out on the bed, smoking, then picked up the telephone. Nan's voice: 'Hello? Hello. Alan, is that you?' Television in the background, the children shouting, his warm, sweet home. Nan would have a hand over one ear, the receiver to the other. 'Where are you, Alan?'

Bradbury replaced the receiver and immediately the telephone rang.

'Nan?'

Reception said his friend was waiting in the bar. No mistaking that starved, bird-boned nape, crowned by the electric frizz.

'Oh, good. I was getting thirsty.'

'What the hell are you doing here?'

She grinned. 'Worked it out. Only one place you'd be, wasn't there? I'll have a pineapple juice.' She was getting some looks in the bar but not as many as he expected – times had changed up here too. 'And I wouldn't mind a pie.'

He put down the glasses and the plate. 'You'll spoil your supper.'

'I like food.'

'So I've noticed.' Bradbury drank. After the pie she had a sausage. 'I'm sorry. I shouldn't have chucked you out like that.' There was something so sure about her, a rootlessness he envied. Living in the south he had been a tree torn out. Not entirely people – not people at all. A certain topography he'd been bred in, he told himself. (Lift up thine eyes to the hills? Hardly. He'd spent half his life getting away and the other half wanting to be back, with hardly an interval between; or so it seemed.)

And now he was here? Nothing.

But for some reason he wished to owe her something.

'I suppose I wanted to be alone. But I'd no right to take it out on you.'

'Could I have another sausage?'

He flung back his head and laughed. He felt in some way redeemed.

The restaurant had gone up in the world, anyway. Spanish waiters, French menu, carafe wine from God-knows-where and candles in bottles. Bradbury loved to watch her eat but she wouldn't touch the wine.

'Why not?'

'Life's a high, isn't it?' She sucked her chicken bone.

Later, over Irish coffee in the residents' bar, 'Where are you going to sleep?'

In the end, he got her a room but at some time in the night she slipped into his, and when Bradbury woke at dawn she was snoring on the floor in the skinny sleeping-bag she kept in her duffle. He'd been dreaming of Nan.

'D'you want to come in here?'

Miranda made love exactly as she ate, with hunger and impersonal pleasure. She didn't kiss much. The smallest breasts he'd ever seen. She knew what she wanted, too. No, she said: like that, here, please? Grinning, her small teeth showing: 'D'you like that?'

'You sound like a bloody waitress.'

'Shut up, lie back and enjoy it.'

'Help, help,' he cried, 'this is rape!'

When they'd finished – or he'd finished with her or she with him – she just curled up and fell into a deep sleep he guessed to be dreamless. By now the city was beginning to form outside the window: the houses and the chimneys and the spires, the factories and guarding hills took shape.

She came up behind him. 'Snow!' she said, and he smiled.

'I thought I hated the stuff. But not this morning. We'll

160

have to get something to put on your feet, though.'

There was a shoe-shop round the corner. He took her measurement and brought back long red boots with ridiculous heels, adding on impulse a short rabbit coat. She accepted them with glee but without thanks, as she took anything given to her – as she herself would have given, if she had anything to give. She stalked around the room, naked but for the jacket and the boots. 'Kinky,' she said. 'Filthy old man.'

They had given up any pretence of looking for a site. They drove to the edge of the moors and here the snow had not melted but lay in streamers between the dark crags. From here you could see seven counties.

'When I was a lad I thought this was where the devil brought Christ.' But he guessed the past meant nothing to her. Why should it?

They sat in the car with Radio One. A file of hikers appeared over the brow of the hill and strode past; they wore stout boots, orange anoraks and in their rucksacks there would be survival packs – tent and emergency rations. You could freeze to death up here.

Miranda wanted to get out. The cold air slapped them in the face. In her long dress, with the red boots and rabbit jacket, and her shawl round her head, she stood in the snow. At that moment the sun came out and fired the town below: all the watching windows to gold, the spires of churches, the silvered slates of the terrace roofs. She walked to the very edge of the scree, where the moors tumbled down, and he watched her.

They went down. He fed her hamburgers in a Wimpy where the drill-hall used to be, then they went to a pub for a whisky for him and she said she wouldn't mind a pasty. 'I've got to have a pee,' she said, 'it's the cold,' and while she was away Bradbury sat over his whisky and listened to the voices around him. Once he saw a man he thought he knew and touched him on the shoulder, but it was a stranger. Well. What had he expected? Welcome back, lad, have a black pudding?

'What's the joke?'

He shook his head.

Bradbury told her – not that she was interested (that was why he told her, because she wasn't interested?) – 'My father was a solicitor. We weren't grand but we were never poor. He grew flowers and cabbages and belonged to the naturalists' society. We always had our own house – quite small, one of those villas, but it wasn't a terrace and our garden was better than most. My mother taught me how to get away, then she didn't want me to leave.'

They climbed up Ropewalk to the castle (no one could budge that, anyway). The centre of the city, where the bus park used to be, had metamorphosed into an improbable piazza. He lost his bearings for a moment, then found the car again and they drove out to the house he had lived in as a child.

At first he thought he had made a mistake, taken a wrong turning, then he realised not. It was a waste and empty space. He sat hunched in the car. Change he'd armed himself for, but not obliteration.

Bradbury got out. It was sleeting now but he walked around bare-headed and here and there could find traces of garden walls, foundations, pavements, hearths, before which people had once sat; even a doorway, intact with frame, hinges and lintel – he pushed it open and beyond, through the door, was the girl laughing at him.

'Do come in,' she said. 'Wipe your feet.'

She danced around to keep warm. Bradbury called after her: 'Here it is! It was here, I think. No – there!' But it couldn't be. The rooms were too small? Or was that an illusion? Even rooms that stood, even new rooms – most of all, new rooms – looked small till you put the furniture in.

You think the houses of your childhood will stand forever. It has nothing to do with whether you were unhappy there, or happy.

Miranda had found a bentwood kitchen chair. 'Do sit down,' she said. 'I'll put the kettle on.'

He stood, his hair rimed with sleet.

'Oh you,' she said. 'You and your past.'

*   *   *

Driving out of town again, they didn't speak. He concentrated on the slippery road, she curled up on the bench seat and seemed to sleep. They drew in at the same spot they had stopped the day before, above the valley. He got out to pee, closing the door quietly, not to wake her. When he got back she was standing outside the car, her duffle bag slung on her shoulder.

'I've never been to Glasgow,' she said. 'Don't fuss – there'll be a lorry.' She kissed his cold mouth, then she was off. A few minutes later a lorry going north stopped and picked her up.

Driving south, going home, Bradbury left the snow behind. When he stopped for coffee, even in the darkness he was aware that the air and the earth were warmer here. Back in the car he twiddled the radio and found a symphony concert from the Festival Hall. He began to sing.

1979

20

A Question of Identity

He stared thoughtfully over the greyish ruin of his oysters at the beautiful woman opposite. It must have been a good lunch. The bones of her ravaged chicken fringed her plate, polished and gleaming as if she had sucked them. The little tongue, remarkably pretty too, was dancing around in her mouth as she questioned the waiter, obviously anticipating already the joys of mousse. He felt an absurd jealousy of the dead, unfeeling chicken which must now be slipping down her throat, and into the lower, mysterious coils of her body; he envied the pile of yellow, flabby mousse, which must soon go the same way. Such a lovely throat would surely conceal the most exquisitely slender oesophagus. He was hopelessly distracted by the slim body, so fragile yet so voracious. He dropped his napkin and peered under the table at her ankles; they were perfect. The only catch in the whole situation seemed to be that he hadn't the faintest idea who she was.

He had lost his memory just as the last obedient oyster slid smoothly down his throat: he remembered its gentle passage, and then he forgot. He supposed she must be with him, and this was confirmed when she said: 'Darling, I think I'll have cream with my mousse.'

He was astonished by the speed with which his mind worked. Perhaps deprived of one important faculty, he would, like the blind, find his other senses remarkably sharpened. He took a quick glance into the mirror opposite. Dark, a little yellow, slightly Spanish he thought; interesting, rather unstable perhaps.

'You look as if you'd never seen your face before,' she laughed. Calm was vital. He knew that memory most often vanished after some fearful experience; such convenient facts seemed to be at his disposal. Perhaps he had committed a murder, and with this possibility in mind, he decided to extemporise. That face was sensitive. He might be important, or at least creative. He drew out his pen – he was pleased to find that it looked expensive – and doodled on the napkin. The results seemed to prove that he was not an artist.

'Darling, what are you doing?' she said. 'Do let me look. Oh, funny stick-men.'

He waved away a hovering waiter. It might be dangerous to eat any more in case he had an allergy. But coffee would be safe, and under the circumstances, a brandy. The dash of fire down his throat revived his reason, and he realised that it was urgent to get away from the lovely creature. She wore a wedding ring, so he supposed she might be his wife. He probably had a job, because he didn't feel the kind of person who did nothing, so surely he could escape. It was half past two. But she could be his secretary. He risked an experiment.'

'Darling, I must be off,' he said.

She raised her lovely eyes in reproach:

'Oh, not yet. After all this is a special occasion.'

There was a hint of conspiracy in her voice, not unpleasant. There must be some bond between them, and if this were true, there would be some record on him of where to find her. There was a champagne bottle on the table, in a bucket, and he peered into it to determine how much he had drunk. The fellow in the glass looked quite sober, but it would be as well to check up.

'Darling, you know we finished it. You said it wasn't the best year.' Some other man, in some other world, might have passed this verdict on the pretty green bottle. He looked at the label, and was relieved to find himself agreeing with this dead or wandering spirit. Obviously some specialised powers were left to him, he was cut off, perhaps mercifully, from only part of his life. It was tempting to follow this companion wherever she might lead him, but it might be safer to retreat to the gentlemen's lavatory.

In the tiled peace of the lavatory he made a pretence of washing his hands. Should he go back and admit his disability? There must have been some deviousness and some independence in his character, because he decided on secrecy for a while. He went into one of the cubicles, and secure at last – at least for the time being – felt it was his home. The tiles in there were the green of young leaves, and a vision passed across his brain of a child climbing a tree to a secret refuge of foliage, this colour, and a voice calling in the orchard below, weak and ridiculous because he was safe. He tried for a moment to put a face to the voice, but a depth of leaves seemed to interrupt. He sank back on the lavatory seat as if onto a welcoming branch, and drew out his wallet. At least he had money – fifty pounds; there was a photograph in the wallet, not the beautiful woman possibly waiting for him still at their table, but a tired anxious face, to which he attributed the voice in the orchard. There were several cards, one printed with a name and address in the City, six engraved with the same name, James Drummond, and an address in Hampstead. Not a bad name. A few minutes later a figure dropped from the window in a quiet street off St James's, landed on a dustbin, and called a cab.

'Just cruise around a bit,' he said.

'These nobs,' thought the cabbie, 'don't know where they're going,' and set off round the park.

Purposely, he had dinner that evening in a crowded restaurant. He had booked in at Brown's, and on the way to dinner bought a newspaper. If he had done something regrettable, it would be as well to know; if he were famous, it might be amusing to find out. But the porter acknowledged his luggage – bought hastily in Piccadilly – with just enough civility and no recognition at all. This impression was confirmed by the paper.

In the restaurant he revelled. He found he enjoyed dining alone, and wondered if this had been a pleasure denied him in the past. At the next table, a couple were quarrelling, a thin, taut pretty girl, and a compact hopeless man. Physically they seemed made for each other, and it was pleasant to think how he was now exempt from this torture; he seemed to know something, in his forgotten memory, of unions which by every physiological and chemical rule should have been perfect, and by human weakness were a prison. He wondered if he was in love with the woman at lunch, but surely there would have been some pull in his body or mind, out of memory, that would not have allowed him to leave by way of the gentlemen's lavatory? He cherished his secret freedom.

The next day he walked around, observing peacefully the hurried crowds. Each member wore on its face a label of haste or desire, or futility. They had all come from something, and were impelled in their progress to return to it, or to pass on. At first he had avoided policemen but now he brazened it out, and was interested to see that his face set off no chase; he was to be left in peace. Perhaps his connection with the woman of yesterday was not, after all, respectable. It was diverting to think that she might have been his mistress, and was but now waiting for the telephone to ring. In the public library he looked for himself in *Who's Who*, and in the Classified; it appeared he was neither a peer of the realm, an actor nor a member of the directly useful professions. He tried a small experiment in the bank – there was a cheque book in his hip pocket.

'Wife and family doing well,' he offered, 'how's yours?' to the clerk who accepted his cheque without question. The matter of signature had been tricky, but a stiff right arm got over that; there was after all no risk – he had still his own face – though the clerk did not look up.

'Having no wife, sir,' replied the clerk, 'I don't have the pleasure of a family.'

The City address he had found in his wallet turned out to be a high building wedged between the great new structures that had sprouted from the ruins. He guessed this was his office, as the name he had taken to be his own was engraved with the address on the card. He had made himself unrecognisable with a pair of enormous sunglasses and a tropical hat, sufficiently out of character, he felt, to conceal his identity. Crouching on a cool stone in the ruins of a graveyard, he watched the office. A man was strolling backwards and forwards behind the window, obviously dictating, peering out now and then directly at the figure on the gravestone. It was amusing to consider what an uproar would have been set up if he had been recognised.

It was late afternoon, and after half an hour's wait black-suited workers emerged, clutching their umbrellas under the cloudless sky, their faces shadowed by bowler hats. The occasional girl brought a flash of colour with a brilliant summer dress, and while the men moved at a quick but precise pace, the women ran, like bright little animals released from a cage. Several of the men held bulging briefcases under their arms. He wondered if he had been one of these, and suspected he had. A small squadron of these ant-like black figures, shadows moving within the shadows, broke off, and filed neatly into a pub on the corner.

He crept closer to the office and peered in. A notice was affixed discreetly by the entrance: 'Dwyer and Drummond'. So he was a partner; just then he heard steps down the stairs, and leant back against the wall, his hat pulled down over his eyes. This must be Dwyer, his briefcase was even more pregnantly bulging, his suit somehow blacker, his umbrella more perfectly furled. He looked worried, which under the circumstances was hardly surprising, but the troughs of anxiety cut in his face seemed permanent. He reminded one of an undertaker. Then, surprisingly, Dwyer smiled to himself, almost giggled, and gave his briefcase a little pat. He wavered for a moment outside the pub, then with a shake of the head, walked off and was lost in the blinding sunset.

The next day there seemed to be an unusual amount of movement in the hotel.

'Not going off for the holiday, sir?' said the reception clerk. Of course it must be the Saturday of August Bank Holiday; he had looked up the date in the newspaper, but this never occurred to him. Out in the street the city was emptying; cars, loaded with luggage, were nosing their way to the sea or the country. Until he realised it was August, the peak of the summer, the heat had seemed pleasant; now it was insufferable.

He understood now the tug there had been from the beginning, or rather from the beginning of memory. He had stood at Swan and Edgar and watched the buses lumbering away to bear their great load north. Once he had joined the queue, but he had realised that in the new routine he had made for himself, it was time for a drink.

Now he found himself panting, like a dog, on the leather seat of a taxi.

'Hampstead,' he said; and looking at the card in his wallet, 'Laurel Road.'

It was good beyond his expectation. Hot with the unfamiliar pressure of the midday sun (his body, faithful in other respects, did not seem to recall the possibilities of temperature), he swayed under the incredible greenness of Laurel Road. He paddled in the pools of shadow under the trees and stared back at a couple who walked, warmly entwined, sweating and oblivious. He leant against the thin towny trunk of a tree, and observed his house.

He saw two children in the garden and instinct recognised them as his own; dizzily he observed a fair head lean from the window to call them in, wearing, out of sight, the ankles he had studied. He found himself divided by the strangest feelings. Inside the house there would be recognition, objects to force their familiarity on him, evidences of a past. There would probably be faces of delight and identification; doubtless some reproach too, but it seemed impossible that he had performed an act which could cut off his welcome, for he was getting to know the man whose clothes he wore and felt pretty certain there was no blood on his hands. Yet it would be possible, though not easy against the currents which drew him to the house, to leave James Drummond behind for good. He wondered who had kept that garden so neat, who had made the decision to paint the front door yellow, what were the names of the children.

Suddenly the girl, for no reason he could see, let out a wail and, sitting down in the flower-bed, began to cry with great gulping, unendurable sobs; the boy, who was older, planted himself stolidly before her, apparently unmoved. It was difficult not to rush in and console her, but he pressed his body back against the tree. After a few minutes the terrible screams ceased as abruptly as they had begun, and the child began methodically to pull off the petals of a rose one by one, cramming them into her podgy fist. The boy now joined in, working his way towards her from the other end of the bed;

when they had collected enough for their private and mysterious purpose, they scrabbled a hole in the soil, and dug the squashed petals in, pressing the earth down with thumps of the fist. The job of destruction done, they forgot it immediately, and he wondered how, as a father, he would have behaved. The boy, who had his own dark colouring, looked impervious to punishment, wirily resistant. The girl, small and fair, seemed too fragile for reproach, but he supposed he must have been able to handle them, though the thought, from where he now stood, was terrifying. Was the pleasure of seeing before you always the witness of your own existence, worth this pain?

Still, when evening came, he knew he would go into the house, and accept whatever identity waited for him. In the dusk the house, with its yellow door and neat lawn, was seductive, the idea of the woman inside with her soft voice and pale hair, even more attractive, desirable enough to blot out the black-suited figure in a high room in the City.

When the sun had set and the house swallowed up the children, to enclose them under cool sheets in a dark room, the man in the shadows moved from under the trees, and began in a strange trot to run up the path. He paused to peer down at the roses; their roots were still secure and they would bloom again. He pushed open the front door, and memory returned with the picture on the wall, which he knew he had never liked, the soft voice calling from the kitchen, which he now understood had, after its first enchantment, bored him for many years, drained him with its monotony until, on their tenth anniversary, his tired mind made its escape. But James Drummond shut the door behind him.

1961

21

No Time for Tigers

It might never have happened, any of it, except of course for the initial catastrophe, had it not been August. Leaving the dry dead city out of season, they had gone, all of them, to Scotland, to Spain, to Frinton, or else they worked their days quickly and disappeared on the earliest train, as though sucked out of the dust by a cleaner suburban air. Only he seemed to be left, in possession of the dark high-ceilinged offices, the tired streets, the empty pubs where the few who remained were solicitous to each other as to invalids, the ailing ones abandoned in a tremendous lethargy. Towards himself he felt a special gentleness and consideration, moving around in his flat with the soft tread of the sickroom attendant.

'You must,' he said, 'look after yourself. You must begin again.' Standing shy as a bride before the mirror he made his vows. 'That body is too white, too plump. It shall have a holiday – very soon.' He fingered again the paper that had weighed in his pocket for one week and six days: ' . . . will work out your notice for a fortnight as from today. Deepest regrets. Hunt.'

For the first few hours he had enjoyed the difference from other men, almost regretted that no friends were there to observe it. 'I am a victim' became an identification, grander than the label on a chain he had carried through the war round his neck. Almost as splendid as the declarations of party, faith or heresy to which he had somehow never found the right. But it had converted, slowly and unkindly, to a pain. He felt marked and supposed that people must point to the sign he surely bore on his forehead. In the papers he saw 'Tiger Escapes', and there, he felt, goes a creature who would understand. Wild and lonely, it was walking the city. Outside its cage, its proper place, it was remarkable but fearful, no longer just another tiger. He wondered vaguely if they would shoot it. Himself, he bore no stripes, no growl, simply his secret which must blaze madly in his eyes.

There was little choice of confidants. So when finally it had to be told, when for the last time he left the office and walked up Holborn, the first friendly face would do as well as any other.

'A double whisky, dear? So you've got the sack. Never mind. You see, you'll show them.'

'I doubt it.'

'Oh, but you will. Water or soda? You see.'

'Younger men, you know. Enterprise and public relations. They've got plans for a PRO.'

'Sounds nasty to me, more like a medicine. It's not the cash, dear?' She nodded from the waist, close but untouchable, hedged by her beer-pulls.

'No, oh no. That's all right. I suppose it's pride. One feels one knows the business.' She was kind, but then that went with the whisky (though nowadays not always). But how could she see as he did? Backwards through days built carefully as a house upon the certainty that the next hour would bring nothing remarkable: or forwards into references tentatively offered.

'Yes, the sack,' he said, as though to speak it would be to exorcise.

'Sometimes it's the best thing. It makes you look around. Excuse me, dear.' She switched on the electric fan, and he watched it grind out painfully a small breeze above their heads.

'It's all bad today,' she said complacently, 'what with the heat, and that tiger.' She looked round nervously as though at any moment the beast might rise snarling from the earth.

'I must be getting back' – although what difference did it make? Except that the last remaining threads of routine would surely soothe and bring some answers.

The flat was much too hot, organised minutely around winter comforts and surprised by the heat. The whisky without food had worked a little, and he decided on a bath, a sandwich and a walk. Now it had betrayed him, he was suddenly curious about the city he had hardly regarded. He felt an unprecedented urge to walk about in it. And he still had the office keys – it would be better to drop them in tonight, than to take them back like a repentant thief on Monday. He thought of Hunt, plump and polished behind his large brown desk, now playing absurdly with his children on a neat, clean beach. 'Hunt here' – that seal-like bark would now be heard by some other man. Did his children dance obediently around him as from the sand he bayed to the stars 'Hunt here'? How in any case could such a man play? He realised that for twenty-five years this idiot phrase had been his anchor; when Hunt was not there the office had seemed frivolous and dangerous, a place of uneasy and unlicensed holiday.

Only now, as he wondered in his bath, did there occur to him the fantastic but delightful possibility of Showing Hunt. He suddenly felt immensely strong, and looked in surprise at his own body, as though it had been borrowed and only recently returned to him. With amazement he clenched his fist on the bar of soap, and for some reason thought again of the tiger. He bared his teeth and stepped out proudly from the bath, holding his breath so that belly became miraculously chest. He stood on his toes, hummed, and flexed his muscles. Never till now had he felt wild, at last he knew that somehow all the small defeated protestations of his life had come together, crying for revenge. For a start he would picnic. Picnic in the evening, eat his sandwiches alone in the warm still evening which was utterly his. He smiled kindly at the gross, overstuffed furniture, pitying it for its ugliness and because it could never understand. It must go, all of it, it was no longer suitable. But later there would be plenty of time for that.

Armed with his new power he walked recklessly in the middle of the road; how beautiful was Montagu Square, a golden rectangle of perfect proportions. The trees seemed more absolutely trees than ever before, the houses shaped by an angel. Before, he had always hurried down Baker Street; now it was a place to linger, to consider with amazement and respect: last outpost of the West End before London crumbled into muddle and politeness in St John's Wood. He pondered a visit to Marylebone, most faded and romantic of stations, forgotten by taxis and patronised only now and then by shy country trains.

But the heart of the city drew him, and he stepped with growing anticipation from Portman Square into Oxford Street. Normally he scurried, nose down, from the great pushing to the greater wind and heat of the Underground. There was still a left-over throb and echo of traffic, but now the number of cars and buses was exactly right in relation to the ugly important street, and he felt welcome and correct taking his place on the pavement. Marble Arch was letting in a sinking sun which cleaned the roads and pointed an irresistible path to St Giles's Circus. He bought a paper, but only to enjoy the remark:

'Lovely evening, such a lovely evening.'

'Nice weather for tigers,' the little man said.

The chase was on. And meanwhile Hunt sat down bravely by the sea, jaws alert, to destroy his last supper; tomorrow, followed by wife and Peter and Pamela, he would take a well chosen train, and Hunt would be Here again. From Regent's Park to Fulham, men in peaked caps raised guns and sticks and possibly nets in a pursuit without direction. Somewhere the beast was walking in the sun, perhaps angry, more likely hungry. He fingered the sandwiches in his pocket.

'Look out love, what a dreamer.' Halfway down Oxford Street the woman skipped sideways, swinging her bags, to avoid the soul who gazed, quite dotty, at the sky.

He loved those resting cranes, that were dragging London up to the sky. This shop and half the city was hauled crazily upwards, every other way out now barred by walls, some more ancient than others. His office (his no longer) was drowned by these great buildings which he loved the more Hunt hated them. In the early stages they crept, all noise in the earth, and Hunt shut every window; then suddenly they climbed the scaffolding, and towered, diminishing all around them. It was forbidden to watch and the small windows became an invitation to delight. Hunt tugged his moustache for fear that the growth outside might dwarf his own labouring expansion, that his small elbowings might be lost in the general push. 'Modernise,' he cried, 'move along the long-servers, the careful and the gentle.'

In Holborn he took a bus, not because he was tired, but to enjoy the city at a different pace. He left it at the viaduct, and walked down Newgate Street. Now it was dusk, but his new certainty told him he must go on, up St Martin's-le-Grand to Aldersgate Street. The streets were empty as a Sunday, but more dangerous, and the old more ominous. Alders, Bishops and New; where, he wondered, had these gates gone, when had they closed and on what? All this he would at last discover, and he looked round, eager as an impassioned tourist, as though expecting the gates themselves to rise at his side, crying their names from the old stones.

At the corner of Falcon Street he stiffened in answer to two quite different calls: one he recognised, mean and curt, from the darkened office of Hunt, Hunt, and Hyer. The other was unfamiliar and impossible to refuse. It spoke to something that had lain sleeping in his mind all evening, and roused to the faintest whisper from the right direction. He followed his feet where they led, not to be contradicted, through the ruins.

The wreck of the Barbican should of all places be haunted, but until tonight he had seen no ghosts. As though recovered from the first shock of obliteration it had seen the worst but was not speaking of it. Now in the darkness which had come down suddenly, a bush seemed a fire, the ceilingless basements populated craters. At the corner of Wood Street he was sure that a hand in his back pushed him towards St Giles. The church seemed to have nothing at all to do with the ruin he had ignored every day: it had taken on the power of a cathedral, and groundsel, weed and bush were subdued before it. They turned in his eye, to point to the door, craning their dusty heads towards some private sun. The notice begging for funds appeared absurdly out of place, the church stronger than any he had seen. All around, the weeds were a kind of grace covering what should not be seen or remembered, but here they lived in the shadow of a building they

175

would never assume to protect. Above the door, hind and saint embraced in an eternal gratitude, forever exchanging shelter and food, everlastingly hospitable.

For some reason he felt no surprise at all, nor fear, that the hunched shadow in the broken chancel should be the tiger.

To feed ham sandwiches to a tiger late at night in a ruined church, normally unlikely, seemed tonight perfectly natural, no more than the conclusion which had called to him in his bath. The animal was obviously petulant, but not unfriendly, and grateful for the sandwiches. As he held out the last, that other call came back, ludicrous but nasty: 'Hunt here.' Around the church, baying under the gentle hind, he felt them circling, closing in with eager cries and bearing between them a gigantic cage. He drew back the sandwich, and stepping carefully backwards led the animal up the aisle. Outside the church they paused, the man watchful, the beast acquiescent. On the other side of London Wall the copper on the beat muttered 'Tigers – what a lark,' but could not see the wonder at his back. In Regent's Park they murmured reassurance. A large cat was mistakenly apprehended west of Sloane Square. In the offices of Hunt, Hunt and Hyer, the beast itself lay down to sleep. No one looked twice at the quiet man who bought a sandwich from the coffee stall, and ate it close on midnight with the air of a picnicker.

On Monday he took a taxi. Nothing less would do for so exceptional a journey. He saw this as his true return. The first had been made in stealth at night; this too must be unobtrusive, but though there could be no applause, the showing of Hunt would surely set off trumpets in his head. It would be splendid, finally and forever justifying all. Nothing, it was quite clear, would ever be the same again, and he had moved through the weekend with a god-like disregard for the habits of his life. He had got up in the afternoon, eaten expensively and left the washing-up. He had slept with his curtains open and wearing no pyjamas. He had dizzied the upstairs cat with salmon and cream and thrown away the Sunday papers without reading them. Stripped to the waist he drank beer in the gardens of Montagu Square.

The crowd was already thick in Aldersgate, and as he slipped quietly through, leaving the taxi, he felt the assurance of a *prima donna incognita*. The fringe were simply hangers-on who would follow any crowd because they queued by instinct. These he disregarded except to say 'excuse me', like the prize-winner who has so far modestly obscured himself, but must now take his reward.

Then 'Ate the curtains they say, horrible havoc, oh horrible'. He had reached the mass of those who knew, and his elbowing became more authoritative. The backs here were solider, more knowing and so less willing.

'The door was locked – how could it get through a locked door?'

'Ah Madam . . . ' he said, but moved on still. He paused for a moment to listen again:

'Wild, quite wild, which just goes to show . . . '; 'used to its cage, fond of its keeper . . . just like a child.'

'Move along, please.'

Then as he turned the corner into Wood Street, slowly like a groan another murmur rolled back in waves through the crowd. Faces were now sharper, keener, children lowered protesting to the ground, and pushing became furtive but more desperate. In panic he thrust into the absolute silence at the front. He broke through just as the fearful bundle was passed down the steps. At one end the shape of the great head lolled in the blanket, at the other the tail hung heavy, forever stilled.

They watched him curiously as a man bereaved, though who in his senses would cry for a tiger? It was after all, dangerous, and this seemed kinder in the end. Much later he climbed the stairs of Hunt, Hunt and Hyer. He had forgotten to return the keys.

1959

22

The Serpent she Loved

'One has been misunderstood.'

'Oh yes, my dear.'

The serpent she loved rearranged himself in the wicker pram he had come to prefer to the basket. From here, as she wheeled him or sat by his side in the autumn sun, he could observe her as she talked – her little teeth, dry, cool skin, amber eyes; her smile for him, her frown for Revelation – while, as for Moses – that monstrous misleader!

'Hush, what have I taught you? Consider Milton. In five minutes a proper reading could correct all misunderstandings. I was sleeping when Satan entered.' His voice was sibilant but she had learned to understand it with remarkable facility after her first surprise, walking in the garden. Thus, each had adapted to the other, although at times the snake was concerned for her sacrifices that brought him such advantage. What was the price to him of minor inconveniences when he could ride high in his pram on a level above the beasts of the field? She must live far from her own kind and, in encounters, dissemble. When she could catch none she had had to shop for mice. An exhausting procedure since she could hardly visit the same pet shop twice. It was the serpent, observing how weary she was from this eccentric marketing, who had conceived the idea of breeding his daily dinner.

'A cage in the attic? Why not?'

'You are so clever.'

The snake smiled. 'They don't call me subtil for nothing.'

'Would you like to go to the end of the spit, to the sea?'

The snake liked the sound of the sea. Not the crash or roar but the shush, the suckling at this flat land on the ebb tide, the bubbling of the mud, the gravelly retreat. The sky was low and wide, the light yellow, at a certain hour of day the susurration of the reeds ceased and unseen birds no longer called. This was a stillness in which anyone who looked out from the cluster of tarred cottages on the other side of the estuary saw the small cloaked figure of the crazy girl with the empty pram. After the first sighting they were not curious. They could see great distances in this country but their eyes turned inward, blankly. Then shuttered windows were blind.

'Should we go back? It's getting late.'

'Hush. Listen. I was Leviathan, you know.'

'I have slept in the bosom of Cleopatra. In Egypt I was properly respected.'

'You told me before. Eat your frog.'

'I am tired.'

'I'll build up the fire. You're just cold.'

'Is winter coming?'

'Oh no, not nearly!'

She watched the firelight on his beautiful scales. She was not repelled by his throat engorged with frog. Indeed, as she had come to know him and grown acquainted with his habits she had found herself embarrassed by her own clumsy eating. How economical to begin digestion already in the mouth, how neat the arrangement by which (so he had explained) the windpipe simply shifted forward to permit breathing while the saliva (a word he preferred to 'venom') got to work.

By comparison how gross her own method appeared! The boiling or browning of flesh that had already been slaughtered on her behalf in ways she preferred not to contemplate. The knife and fork, the cutting up, the inelegant chewing in a carious mouth she had begun to see as a most unpleasing orifice. And then the detritus, the plates to be scraped and washed.

When she was first struck by the inelegance of human eating, she took her meals quickly in the kitchen out of sight of her fastidious friend. Lately and secretly she had been experimenting and tonight for the first time in his presence popped a small piece of raw liver into her mouth, held it there, closed her eyes and forced herself to swallow.

'Please don't watch.' As a tree-snake his eyesight was good.

'You wouldn't prefer a frog?'

'That's very kind but I'm not sure I could manage it.'

'Possibly you are not carnivorous.'

'I do prefer vegetables.'

He had a quick tongue. She had her pride. So it was only when she believed him to be sleeping on the climbing frame she had set up by her chair that she allowed herself to dwell on her failure.

'Why are your eyes wet?'

'I thought you were asleep.'

'Are you about to shed your skin?'

'Oh, snake, how I wish I could! I am weeping because I would be as you in all ways.'

His tail embraced her neck as he lay coiled in her lap.

'Hush! Each to his own nature. It is my snakeness you love, your womanliness I cherish.'

'But God,' she said, ashamed.

'Was wrongly reported. See – there is no enmity between us. Serpent and woman have always been compatible. Children, you will have observed, have no fear of snakes until they are taught to fear. In lands where Moses holds no sway, we are cherished. There I am known as Ejo. Call me that, if you like.'

'My name is Eva.'

'A remarkable coincidence, though I daresay it means nothing. It is cool between your breasts. May I lie there?'

'Please do!'

Winter – and her fear of it for Ejo – for a time withdrew and the flat eel-country woke up one morning and found itself turned to gold. Even the mud of the saltings was gilded and pools blinked at a blue-eyed sky.

From a great distance a figure was approaching.

The earth was warm enough from its hoarded summer for the girl and the serpent to play in the orchard.

On their bellies they wriggled and raced through the

crisply toasted leaves. Ejo won, of course. However hard she worked her elbows and her knees Eva arrived at the king of trees – the richest Worcester of the reddest fruit – to find him already hiding among the fallen waspy apples or coiled on a branch.

'Snake!' she cried, laughed and flung off her clothes.

Now she was almost like him. On glass she would have been helpless as he but on the uneven earth her nakedness together with her greater reach would have made her the winner but for her fear of wasps. Her breasts, her thighs, the little mound of Venus versus his sidewinding (learned long ago from the viper in the desert) very nearly cut the odds to equal. Though her movements were those of an awkward swimmer and she was dreadfully scratched by brambles.

'I have seen something like that before,' said the snake. 'The reptile from the primeval waters taking its first walk on land. I advised against it.

'I used to have legs,' said the snake, 'but I gave them up. Pointless appendages.'

'You are perfect as you are,' she breathed and together they rested in the garden and played. His particular gift was self-concealment and more than once she feared that she had lost him forever and then a mossy branch gave the sibilant hiss she had come to know as laughter.

In those days of Indian summer Eva cast off shame with her clothes and walked naked in the orchard. Ejo caught his own frogs from the pool. In winter, they agreed, the bath could be converted to a tank.

Once, she imagined she had caught a glimpse of two figures halfway along the causeway through the flats. But the light in these parts was hallucinatory. On a hot summer day she had seen a ship in the sky. A man waving might be one of the few sparse trees. Or a crow.

'I am so happy,' she said by the fire at night, munching an apple.

'Happy as Eve,' said the serpent, coiled around her waist, the sweetest belt she had ever known.

'But surely Eve – ?'

'Another calumny. Adam was the fool, not to be grateful.

For form's sake I acknowledge Satan but the truth is, it was mostly my work. And Eve's. Without that first apple you would not be happy now.'

'But the Fall?'

'A wicked rumour perpetuated by those with a vested interest in guilt. How could their first innocence have been bliss, since in ignorance one does not know that one is blissful? After Eden they had a few bad patches but nothing's for free.'

'So the whole story – ?'

'Propaganda. Blatant discrimination against serpents and women. God made Eve first anyway. Adam was an afterthought, the brainstorm of a tired creator. A pretty slapdash one too, as your liberation movement has finally grasped. I mean, who in their right mind would wear their genitals outside?' The snake quivered with distaste in his own delicious way – a contraction of every muscle from tail to handsome head that shone sometimes green, sometimes brown, by firelight pure gold. 'You don't. I don't.'

'Ejo? You are not by any chance gay?'

'Certainly not! I believe we must propagate as best we can. Though an ideal future would lie in androgynous parthenogenesis. Who wants that idiot's seed anyway?'

'I think there is some work in that direction,' Eva mused. 'Though I understand the primitive system is quite pleasurable.'

'You want pleasure? Just let me get this mouse down and I'll show you.'

How gently the blunt nose searched, teasing, probing, loving, the tail at work too until Eva sang with joy all through that night; and at last before the dead fire they lay so twined it was hard to tell which was serpent and which woman. Were it not for the limitations of their species, Ejo–Eva would have been born, serpent-woman.

Perhaps she sang too loud or in this eel country the men who gathered with their tarred brands around the cottage could snuff out a snake. By the morning winter was back and they crouched hunchbacked, crippled trees that have always grown as they are because gravity is heavier here and the sky presses and between the two sleet is carried on a wicked wind.

*   *   *

Ejo said: 'I shall need a hibernaculum.' But his voice was faint and his eyes were milky.

Eva stoked the fire and bolted the door. His poor skin was dull, all shine gone and it seemed to her that he must be dying.

'There! See – the fire.'

'I am blind.'

The skin was splitting at the edges of Ejo's lips.

In the evening they lit their brands.

'Why do they hate us?' she said.

'Because we are sisters. The greatest offence against man is not the serpent but the friendship of women. It was the same in the Garden.'

'Ejo?'

'A goddess. Just a name among many. I've been wor-shipped as often as I've been bad-mouthed.'

'Hush. You must rest.'

The crazy girl pulled on her boots and her cloak, wrapped her serpent in a shawl, laid it tenderly in the wicker pram and the two made their escape through the wicket gate at the eastern end of the garden.

Ejo sloughed her skin.

Eva moved to the city.

They live happily now in the parlour behind the pet-shop at a temperature thermostatically controlled not to rise above 40 degrees centigrade. They give no trouble to anyone and no one bothers them.

1990

23

The Noise from the Zoo

From where he dug in the night Felix could hear the zoo. As
the last visitor left the murmur began; these were the smaller,
familiar animals, the gossips, but by midnight the larger and
the rarer gave voice and Felix paused to listen to the bellows,
moans of complaint, and wild laughter. At first this seemed
to him an hysterical conversation between insomniacs, later,
as weariness and fancy overtook him, the Passion of the
beasts, the desperate cry of martyred innocents. He did not
care for zoos. The animals appeared to him prisoners without hope of release or redemption. Those not captured but
born there were like the blind born without sight. For himself, if he were a beast and could choose he would prefer
capture, if only to have something to remember, to talk about
at night.

He rested a while and opened his sandwiches and flask. A
policeman loomed out of the dark. Felix held his breath. The
policeman took in the dim red lamp, the shovel, and the low
barricade around the growing hole.

'Fine night for it. On your own?'

Felix nodded and offered him coffee. They drank. The
policeman walked on. First he looked over the barricade:

'You've got a good hole there.'

When he had finished Felix tidied up, took the shovel but
left the barricades and the lamp. Eventually someone would
probably take them away. Meanwhile the hole was deep
enough but not so deep a running child or an unwary adult
falling in, might harm themselves. That was important. That

184

was part of the plan, just as it was to Felix of no significance that the hole would sooner or later be filled in. He hurried home and at seven o'clock woke his wife, Audrey, with a cup of tea.

Audrey said for the tenth time: 'What do you mean, a hole?'

Her brother, Gerald, shifted the pipe in his teeth. 'He means what he says, Aud. A hole.' He drew in to the kerb and parked. He added: 'Is a hole.'

'That's what I meant,' said Felix.

The hole had not yet come to official notice, or if it had, was assumed to be to some public purpose. The lamp and the barricades declared its right to be there. It was a fine Saturday morning in the park. Some women were sitting by the hole in deckchairs. They called to their children to come away from the edge. A tramp spat in the hole. A couple of girls laughed at it. Audrey looked at it sideways, not to be caught out. Gerald planted himself in front of it.

'It's quite a small hole.'

'It's big,' said Audrey sharply, 'it's far too big.'

Gerald twinkled: 'Too big what for?'

'Don't encourage him,' she snapped. 'He's mad.'

'Well,' Gerald repeated, turning to Felix, 'what for?'

'Nothing.'

'Why?'

'For no reason.' Felix averted his eyes from the hole. He was determined that it should be pointless. If he looked too long he might be moved by it, was aware already of stirrings of pride as people paused to peer in.

When they got back to the car Audrey was waiting, tense, ready to cry. At home, without Gerald, who had gone off laughing and wagging his head, she turned to Felix:

'How can you do a thing like that for no reason? Are you mad? What do you hope to gain by it?'

'Nothing.'

'Then what? Do you *want* to get into trouble?'

'Certainly not.'

She gave him a wild, white look and began to sob. 'If you wanted a hole you could have had one *here*!'

He was disturbed, troubled for the first time since he

thought of the hole. He began to see the danger. He spread his hands: 'Don't you see, it wouldn't have done? Here, in our garden, where we live, it would have meant something. It would have had a reason, a consequence. The essence is its pointlessness, that is its beauty.' He pondered, got himself a beer and took it into the garden. He had chosen a hole because it was empty, meaningless, the perfect, motiveless act. Yet already the policeman had described it as good, Audrey said it was big, Gerald small. He himself had spoken of beauty. He wondered. For the first time he cared for the hole, wished to run and protect it from corruption, interpretation. It would be better it should be filled, even that. He hurried to save his hole.

He took a risk, going in daylight. He had thrown in only half a shovelful of earth when authority, at last awakened, tapped him on the shoulder.

'I didn't want to hurt anyone. I don't believe in violence. I wanted to prove something.'

'?'

'That an act is possible, in itself, without motive or consequence. The relief of something pure that couldn't be spoiled. Objective, without past or future. I have a good job. I love my wife. She had nothing to do with this.'

The hole was not at once filled in. It became at first somewhere to go on a bright evening where the children could play, then a kind of shrine. Larger barricades were put up because of the danger that the walls might cave in. The police measured it. It appeared on television. People began to throw in flowers, even coins. They stood around in knots as if they expected something to happen. It became a famous spot for harmless lunatics, preachers and lovers.

Those who questioned Felix were inclined at first to be lenient, to dismiss him as a harmless nut. He was consistently calm and polite, was revealed through investigation to have been, up to now, an entirely respectable citizen, modestly ambitious, reasonably successful. And after all, it was only a hole.

The Inspector considered himself a bit of a liberal. He had

met most sorts and while it was his job to bring them to book he had experienced, more than once, a twinge of sympathy for the antisocial. He admitted to Felix:

'These youngsters, they're not the only ones who can't stomach what's going on. Your conformist society. Your welfare state.' He twinkled. 'There are times when I've felt like chucking a brick myself. We've had most things, but I must admit we've never had a hole.'

Felix smiled. They had several such one-sided conversations. The weather grew hot. The Inspector sweated. He was aware of neglecting his other duties. He became obsessed with the hole. He dreamed of it as a vacancy into which he might fall. He walked with his eyes cast down. He was afraid to sleep.

It was August, the silly season. In other parts of London holes began to appear overnight. Some revealed subterranean streams, archeological remains, or the bones of those who had died by violence in war or by stealth. Some, like Felix's, were empty.

Felix's case came up, he paid a small fine. The magistrate asked if a psychiatric report had been made. It had. Felix was sane. But for the mysterious notoriety the hole had achieved, this would have been the end of the affair. As he left the court Gerald took his elbow:

'You'd better duck into the car double quick.' A quarrelsome crowd had gathered. A man carrying a placard inscribed KEEP THE HOLE was hit by a tomato. A woman screamed. The police arrived to break them up and Felix slipped away unobserved.

'I never meant this to happen,' Felix explained that evening to the Inspector. The Inspector arrived on foot, in civilian clothes. He looked unfamiliar, as if he might be wearing a disguise, and very tired. They sat in deckchairs in the garden and drank beer.

'If you could explain it,' said the Inspector. 'If you could say you were looking for something.'

'I wasn't.'

The Inspector nodded glumly.

'If you had buried something or heard of something buried . . .'

187

'No.'

The Inspector sighed.

'I have dreams.'

'You need a holiday.'

Felix had grown to like the Inspector. He wished he could help him.

'Now look here, old chap,' said Gerald, 'this has got to stop. It's making Aud ill. Enough is enough.'

'It's out of my hands,' said Felix. That night he was woken by her crying. He touched her shoulder but she curled away, drawing her knees up to her chin. She had grown thin and her shoulders were sharp. The bones cut her flesh like knives. At last she said:

'I don't see why you had to do it. You had everything.'

'It is the only thing I have done in my life.'

'But it has brought nothing but trouble.'

'It has been misunderstood.'

They lay for a while, before they slept, fingers touching in the dark.

The Inspector had got into the habit of calling most evenings. When he appeared Audrey shut herself in the kitchen. As they paced the garden she watched, a pale, wavering shape in the window.

The Inspector looked at the lettuces.

'You've never thought, there might be a reason, something you've forgotten? The kind of thing the trick cyclists dig up?'

'No.'

The Inspector shook his head. 'I go along with them there. I've read a bit. Everything we do has a motive. What do you see in the hole?'

'Nothing.' As if to reassure himself Felix repeated: 'Nothing.'

As he left the Inspector said:

'Had you heard? They're going to fill it in.'

The workmen sent by the Parks Committee to fill it in were met by a hostile crowd. A Save the Hole group had been formed and this demonstration was clearly well organised. Some carried placards bearing Felix's picture and the slogan: AN ENGLISHMAN'S HOLE IS HIS CASTLE. Some had actually climbed the barricades and settled in the hole with sand-wiches. The police arrived. There was a scuffle. The squat-ters in the hole refused to budge and the police did not bother to lift them out. After all, it was only a hole. The workmen retreated.

That night there was a torchlight procession. Each hole was visited from the City through Pimlico to Chelsea then north to the park. They sang quietly as they marched and Felix watched with fear and wonder as they approached, the brands flickering among the trees. Leading them was the Inspector, wild-eyed, his head thrown back like a prophet. He did not see Felix. His gaze was fixed on the point where, from the direction of the zoo, the police came with shovels.

The marchers tore down the barricades. No one ever knew who threw the stone but it hit the Inspector on the temple. With a look of surprise he swayed and toppled into the hole. Fights broke out. A passing and oblivious dog, his mind perhaps on burying bones, paused, was astonished by the hole and set up a piercing howl. From the zoo a hyena answered. One man seized a brand and set fire to his cloth-ing. Then a fine rain, the first for weeks, began to fall.

When the crowd had been dispersed and the injured car-ried away Felix, who was not the kind of man you would notice in a riot, came out from the trees and stood by the hole. He hardly recognised it. In the fighting the edges had been broken and it had already begun to fill with rain. He saw it, thinking of the Inspector, as a grave; soon it would be a pond. If you looked long enough you could make anything you liked of it. Someone had left a lamp. Kneeling, the rain trickling down his neck, he held it close to the rising surface of the water and saw, reflected, a face he recognised to be his own. He stood, awkwardly, and found that he was crying. He stayed for a while listening to the noise from the zoo.

1972

JANICE ELLIOTT

NECESSARY RITES

To Moira Frankland, writer of fairy tales, all seems in order for Christmas: her marriage works, her teenage son is reasonably civilised, and she has agreed to take in a homeless waif over the holiday. But ten years ago the couple's daughter drowned, leaving deep, unresolved grief. Her husband's MoD contract becomes worryingly sinister, and the presence of a strange girl in the house proves just as disturbing. Only young Sam perceives that his parents are making a terrible mistake.

'Achieves the tantalising dovetail between literal and metaphorical, inner and outer, that is typical of Elliott's literary agility . . . The kind of magic she always gives . . . imbues even a menacing futuristic world with beauty as well as danger'
Times Literary Supplement

'Janice Elliott is always perceptive, inventive, stylish . . . The freshness is in the adroit interlocking of the domestic and political, realistic and imaginative, childhood and maturity, through finely controlled evocation and imagery'
Daily Telegraph

'Elliott has skilfully woven the troubled state of the family with that of the nation'
Options

'The language is spare, taut and vivid . . . no opportunity for significance is wasted'
The Scotsman

'One of the most resourceful and imaginative living English novelists'
Paul Bailey

JANICE ELLIOTT

LIFE ON THE NILE

'The kind of novel at which Janice Elliott excels – formal,
literary, compassionate'
The Times Literary Supplement

'A mystery story on several levels which Elliott probes with the
delicacy of an archaeologist . . . As you read the quiet title fills
with colour and noise and acquires meaning. The physical sense
of Egypt is directly, unobtrusively conveyed . . . The air is full
of shadows and echoes'
Candia McWilliam in The Glasgow Herald

'The plot rolls from revelation to revelation until the truth has
its cathartic effect. This is a stylish and imaginative book,
concerned with death but also full of life'
The Sunday Times

sceptre